A Short History of Indians in Canada

OTHER BOOKS BY THOMAS KING
PUBLISHED BY THE UNIVERSITY OF MINNESOTA PRESS

*The Inconvenient Indian: A Curious Account
of Native People in North America*

One Good Story, That One: Stories

The Truth About Stories: A Native Narrative

Thomas King

A Short History of Indians in Canada

STORIES

University of Minnesota Press

MINNEAPOLIS

Originally published in 2005 by HarperCollins Publishers Ltd.

First published in 2013 in the United States by the University of Minnesota Press

Published by the University of Minnesota Press
111 Third Avenue South, Suite 290
Minneapolis, MN 55401-2520
http://www.upress.umn.edu

A Cataloging-in-Publication record for this book is available from the Library of Congress.

Printed in the United States of America on acid-free paper
The University of Minnesota is an equal-opportunity educator and employer.

20 19 18 17 16 15 14 13   10 9 8 7 6 5 4 3 2 1

For Floyd O'Neil and Leroy Little Bear,
who took the time

A Short History of Indians in Canada

Can't sleep, Bob Haynie tells the doorman at the King Eddie. Can't sleep, can't sleep.

First time in Toronto? says the doorman.

Yes, says Bob.

Businessman?

Yes.

Looking for some excitement?

Yes.

Bay Street, sir, says the doorman.

Bob Haynie catches a cab to Bay Street at three in the morning. He loves the smell of concrete. He loves the look of city lights. He loves the sound of skyscrapers.

Bay Street.

Smack!

Bob looks up just in time to see a flock of Indians fly into the side of the building.

Smack! Smack!

Bob looks up just in time to get out of the way.

Whup!

An Indian hits the pavement in front of him.

Whup! Whup!

Two Indians hit the pavement behind him

Holy Cow! shouts Bob, and he leaps out of the way of the falling Indians.

Whup! Whup! Whup!

Bob throws his hands over his head and dashes into the street. And is almost hit by a city truck.

Honk!

Two men jump out of the truck. Hi, I'm Bill. Hi, I'm Rudy.

Hi, I'm Bob.

Businessman? says Bill.

Yes.

First time in Toronto? says Rudy.

Yes.

Whup! Whup! Whup!

Look out! Bob shouts. There are Indians flying into the skyscrapers and falling on the sidewalk.

Whup!

Mohawk, says Bill.

Whup! Whup!

Couple of Cree over here, says Rudy.

Amazing, says Bob. How can you tell?

By the feathers, says Bill. We got a book.

It's our job, says Rudy.

Whup!

Bob looks around. What's this one? he says.

Holy! says Bill. Holy! says Rudy.

Check the book, says Bill. Just to be sure.

Flip, flip, flip.

Navajo!

Bill and Rudy put their arms around Bob. A Navajo! Don't normally see Navajos this far north. Don't normally see Navajos this far east.

Is she dead? says Bob

Nope, says Bill. Just stunned.

Most of them are just stunned, says Rudy.

Some people never see this, says Bill. One of nature's mysteries. A natural phenomenon.

They're nomadic you know, says Rudy. And migratory.

Toronto's in the middle of the flyway, says Bill. The lights attract them.

Bob counts the bodies. Seventy-three. No. Seventy-four. What can I do to help?

Not much that anyone can do, says Bill. We tried turning off the lights in the buildings.

We tried broadcasting loud music from the roofs, says Rudy.

Rubber owls? asks Bob.

It's a real problem this time of the year, says Bill.

Whup! Whup! Whup!

Bill and Rudy pull green plastic bags out of their pockets and try to find the open ends.

The dead ones we bag, says Rudy.

The lives ones we tag, says Bill. Take them to the shelter. Nurse them back to health. Release them in the wild.

Amazing, says Bob.

A few wander off dazed and injured. If we don't find them right away, they don't stand a chance.

Amazing, says Bob.

You're one lucky guy, says Bill. In another couple of weeks, they'll be gone.

A family from Alberta came through last week and didn't even see an Ojibway, says Rudy.

Your first time in Toronto? says Bill.

It's a great town, says Bob. You're doing a great job.

Whup!

Don't worry, says Rudy. By the time the commuters show up, you'll never even know the Indians were here.

Bob catches a cab back to the King Eddie and shakes the doorman's hand. I saw the Indians, he says.

Thought you'd enjoy that, sir, says the doorman.

Thank you, says Bob. It was spectacular.

Not like the old days. The doorman sighs and looks up into the night. In the old days, when they came through, they would black out the entire sky.

Tidings of Comfort and Joy

It was beginning to look a lot like Christmas, and the winter storm that drifted through the Caledon Hills during the night should have raised Hudson Gold's spirits. Winter was, after all, his favourite season, and he was always delighted with the first snow, with the way it lay on the dense firs thick as frosting, with the way the bare branches of the birches and the maples wrapped themselves in ice and flashed like cut crystal in the cold light. Even the dark, dank beaver ponds that Eleanor had imported all the way from Cleveland looked crisp and festive.

And Hudson was especially fond of Christmas, looked forward to the clamour of roasts, mashed yams, and pies, to the sharp taste of bittersweet chocolates from Belgium, to the tart and juicy clementines from Morocco, eagerly sought the hearty and well-met company of friends and neighbours, waited anxiously for the ritual give and take of gift-giving.

Hudson was, in fact, an especially skilled and considerate gift-giver. Year after year, he took great delight in surprising Eleanor with thoughtful presents. A fur stole. A cruise to St. Croix. An eight-piece set of hand-painted antique wine glasses. A designer raincoat.

"Well Hudson," Eleanor would say each time she opened a present, "you've done it again."

And he liked to receive gifts, could remember what someone had given him years after the fact. When he was four, his parents put a red and yellow train under the Christmas tree. When he was five, they came home with a puppy. He could still remember that.

But, today—the day before Christmas—as Hudson stood by the bay window and looked out at the trees and the ponds, and the tipis in the small valley below the main house, he was harassed by a growing feeling of unease.

Hudson had read about people who became depressed in December, who were so overwhelmed by the expectations of the season and of their families, were so convinced of their own worthlessness, that they either went on a killing spree or strung themselves up by their belt in a closet. Rich, poor, it didn't seem to matter, though Hudson guessed that rich people, in general, coped with Christmas better than poor ones.

But Hudson knew it wasn't the season and it wasn't the weather. It was the Indians.

During the sixties and seventies and for the first half of the eighties, collecting Indians had been the rage with most of the families in the Caledon Hills. And while most everyone had since moved on to newer enthusiasms such as exotic pets, rain-forest acreages, and internet stocks, Hudson stayed the course and had, over the years, put together one of the more impressive collections of Indians east of Saskatoon.

It was Eleanor who bought him his first Indian, a Seminole that she had run across in a small shop in Clinton, Oklahoma. The next year, Franklin Spense, of all people, his neighbour on the other side of the ridge, a gun enthusiast and a stickler for the sanctity of property lines, gave him an Ojibway shaman. The year after that, Vince Muir, whose family at one time had owned all the land in Caledon Hills, brought over a Mohican that he had picked up at a yard sale.

"I thought Mohicans were extinct."

"That was the rumour, but they found a bunch of them in northern Massachusetts a couple of years back," said Vince. "Don't worry, he's authentic."

Hudson hadn't really planned to collect Indians, and he had never really gone out of his way to locate new pieces, at least not the way Jack Cartier and his wife Bridget chased after Hummel figurines. It was true he had travelled all the way to Quebec City to purchase a set of four Cheyenne Dog Soldiers, but that had been more for investment than for mere collecting.

Eleanor, at least in the beginning, had been the real force behind the collection. For his fifty-sixth birthday, she bought him seven tipis and a video on how to set up an authentic Indian camp. And then, last Christmas, she had come back from Alberta with a matched drum team—eight singers, a buffalo-skin drum, and a pow-wow song book with a CD, so you could learn the songs and sing along if you felt like it. The singers were an absolutely stunning gift, even better than the Dog Soldiers.

Of course the singers weren't perfectly matched. The lead singer was a little on the heavy side and two of the Indians didn't look as Indian as Hudson would have hoped.

"I raised that question with the dealer," Eleanor told him, "and he said that every one of them has a status card."

"Those two aren't quite as dark as the others." Hudson felt bad about raising the matter. "And only three of them have long hair."

"Honey, be reasonable," said Eleanor, "it's almost impossible to find a matched set of full bloods, anymore."

Hudson enjoyed listening to the drum, but, so far as he could discern, Indian music had only two kinds of beats, a regular four-four beat and a slightly syncopated one-two rhythm that sounded a little like someone shuffling along on a bad leg. Both of these, Hudson suspected, could become monotonous.

The voices, on the other hand, were anything but monotonous. They were high-pitched, energetic, and shrill, almost irritating. Franklin said it brought to mind Eastern Orthodox chanting, while Vince's wife, Edna, said it reminded her of the Maori in New Zealand. Except the Maori did more shouting. And stomping.

Hudson found that if he listened to the drumming and the singing too long, the music gave him a headache.

"Still," Eleanor told him, "I wouldn't dismiss it out of

hand. Remember you didn't like progressive jazz at first, either."

Almost before he knew it, Hudson had acquired several dozen Indians. Most of these had been gifts. A few such as the Dog Soldiers were purchases, while four or five—he forgot the exact number—had been dropped over his fence in gunny sacks. Not that he minded. It had been fun playing with the Indians, placing them around the property, figuring out where each grouping should go. Lakota in the open. Cherokee in the hills above the house. Mohawk down by the pond. Chickasaw and Choctaw in the trees.

Mind you, maintaining the collection hadn't been cheap. Even though he had encouraged the Indians to augment their diet through gathering, the cost of the food alone had been an unpleasant shock. Hudson considered allowing them to hunt, but Vince had talked him out of it.

"In the first place, there's nothing left to hunt," Vince told him over a glass of wine one evening. "And if your Indians go wandering over to Bob Philips' place and mistake one of his prize sheep for a large dog or butcher one of Arthur Dobbs' cows because it looks like a buffalo, you'll never hear the end of it."

And there were the grooming costs—he had been lucky to find someone who would come out so he didn't have to take the Indians in to town—and the clothing repairs—even the buckskin that the Indians came with wore out over time—and cords of firewood—Hudson couldn't have the Indians chopping down his trees—not to mention the nutritional supplements needed to keep the collection healthy and alert. He'd considered renting half a dozen porta-potties, but, in the end, decided that letting the Indians dig their own holes was more authentic, wouldn't harm the environment in any noticeable way, and gave them something to occupy their time. For a brief period he had worried about the amount of exercise the Indians were getting and had dragged an old NordicTrack out of the basement and left it at the edge of the valley, but so far as he knew, none of the Indians had ever given it a try. In the end, he reasoned, living outdoors and foraging was probably exercise enough.

The problem, and Hudson wasn't sure this was the right word to use, had surfaced the day before. He was having breakfast in the kitchen when he noticed an Indian down by one of the beaver ponds. Hudson walked to the window for a better look. From a distance Hudson couldn't be sure, but the binoculars that he kept on the window ledge in case the Indians did anything interesting confirmed what had been, up to that moment, unthinkable.

A woman. He couldn't tell if it was one of the two Blackfoot that he had picked up at auction on the internet or if it was the Cree maiden that his brother Bert had sent them for their thirtieth anniversary.

What he *was* sure of, now that he had the binoculars in focus, was that the woman was pregnant. Not a little pregnant. Very pregnant. So pregnant in fact that Hudson was obliged to pull up a chair and sit on it before he fell down.

He lowered the binoculars and practised rhythmic breathing until the lightheadedness went away. Then he slowly raised the binoculars to his eyes. It took him a minute to find the woman again. But, yes, damn it, she was pregnant all right. Hudson put the tips of his fingers in his nose and tried to think. How in the world had she managed to get pregnant? What kind of reputable dealer would sell an Indian who hadn't been fixed? God, if he ever figured out where this particular piece had come from, there would be hell to pay.

"Eleanor!"

Hudson called his wife four times, annoyed that she didn't answer, and it was only when he opened his mouth a fifth time to really shout at her that he remembered that she had gone to Toronto to spend Christmas Eve with her sister and wouldn't be back until late Christmas Day.

"Great," Hudson said to no one in particular. "Just great."

That night the Indians began singing. Hudson tried listening for a while, tried for the hundredth time to catch a glimpse of a recognizable melody in the drumming, but, in the end, gave up and turned on the television. The golf channel had an interesting show on short-game shots and lag putts, and there was a James Bond movie he had seen six or seven times before but which was still entertaining. He thought about phoning Eleanor, but she would only worry and insist on coming home.

The next morning he called Vince and told him what had happened. "Jesus, Hudson," said Vince after

Hudson had told him the story for the third time. "You haven't been . . . you know."

"Of course not," said Hudson, trying to sharpen his voice, but finding himself pleased, in a small way, that Vince would even think such a thing of him.

"Then you could have a serious problem," said Vince. "You ever see *Jurassic Park*?"

"So, what do you think I should do?"

"I'll swing by and pick up Franklin," said Vince. "Just don't go down there alone."

Hudson busied himself for the next hour or so, laying out the Christmas treats that Eleanor had made in case company came by while she was gone. Miniature pumpkin pies, mincemeat tarts, fruit cake, chocolate cherry cordials, mulled wine, and Italian salami on Wheat Thins. He loaded the CD player, sprayed the pine scent around the doorways, and turned up the heat just a little so that, when Vince and Franklin finally arrived, the house had a warm and festive air to it.

"Since neither of you knows how to shoot," said Franklin, dragging the black, ballistic-nylon bags into the kitchen, "I brought the shotguns."

"Here you go," said Vince, and he handed Hudson a gift-wrapped package. "Merry Christmas. It's golf balls. I never know what to get you."

"Have some tarts," said Hudson, humming along to the music. "The wine's on the stove."

Franklin walked to the window and looked out. The sun had settled in behind the edge of the escarpment and the light slowly disappeared. "You say you saw her down by the beaver ponds?"

"That's right."

"And she was pregnant?" Franklin kneeled down and unzipped the gun cases.

"Very."

"You think it's one of those parthenogenesis things?" said Vince.

"Only happens with plants and certain insects," said Franklin, "You want the double barrel or the over-under?"

The trail down to the Indian camp was clogged with ferns and nettles and cedar bush. Hudson suggested they use flashlights, but Franklin argued they should maintain the element of surprise.

"They're friendly," said Hudson. "No one sells hostiles anymore."

"I don't know," said Vince, "remember that Haida that the Ruperts bought."

As the three men reached a stand of trees just above the camp, the drumming started up again as it had the night before. "This is good," said Franklin. "They won't hear us over that noise."

Hudson could see the camp clearly now. The drummers were singing. The women were sitting on the grass at the edge of a fire, their blankets pulled around them for warmth. It was a peaceful scene, thought Hudson, like something you'd see in a painting. Or in a department store window.

"Christ," said Franklin, "are those Bob's sheep?"

"Holy," said Vince, leaning on Hudson's shoulder, "Art's going to blow a gasket."

At the back of the camp, in a small corral, near a large, well-lit tipi, were several sheep and two cows. Further back in the shadows, other shapes moved.

"Deer?" said Franklin. "Where the hell did deer come from?"

"Jesus," said Vince, "the place is a damn zoo."

"You know what it looks like," said Hudson who still had Christmas music playing in his head. "It sort of looks like a nativity scene."

"Right," said Franklin, "and we're the three wise men."

"You see the woman?" said Vince.

"I'm guessing she's in that big tipi," said Hudson.

"Okay," said Vince. "So, what do you want to do?"

"Come on," said Hudson, who was humming 'Jingle Bells' under his breath, "let's go say, hello." And before Vince or Franklin could stop him, he stepped out of the trees and headed down the hill for the camp.

Several of the Indians looked up when Hudson strode into the camp, the shotgun resting comfortably in the crook of his arm. "Merry Christmas," he said, smiling and nodding his head at no one in particular. "And a Happy New Year." Hudson could hear Vince and Franklin struggling behind him, but he didn't wait for them to catch up. He walked straight to the tipi.

Franklin walked straight to the corral. "They're Bob's sheep, all right."

"Hey, Franklin," said Vince. "Come look at this."

Hudson and Vince and Franklin stood at the entrance to the tipi and looked in. The woman was lying on a pile of furs, and on either side of her lay a baby.

"Twins," said Vince. "You lucky bastard." And he whacked Hudson on the shoulder. "Now those are collectible."

The men stood and watched the scene in silence. Finally Franklin took out his handkerchief and blew his nose. "They sure are cute."

"Don't tell Edna," said Vince. "She'll want to take them both home."

"Too bad they grow up," said Franklin.

Hudson could feel tears welling up in his eyes, but as he watched one of the babies roll over and begin nursing, he realized, with a start, that he hadn't brought anything to give the Indians. Not that he had ever given them anything, but tonight was special. Christmas Eve and two new babies. A moment to be commemorated, to be remembered. He patted his pockets, and then slowly, softly at first, and then more loudly, he began singing, "Angels we have heard on high . . ." At first, Vince and Franklin weren't sure what to do, but Hudson nodded to each man in turn and they joined in at the chorus.

And when they finished the first song, before Franklin or Vince could say anything, Hudson, almost without taking a breath, went right into "Good King Wenceslas" and then on to "Silent Night," "Oh Little Town of Bethlehem," "Away in a Manger," and "Frosty the Snowman."

It was late by the time they left the camp, but Hudson didn't feel tired in the least. He was elated, filled with almost more Christmas spirit than he could contain. His only regret was that Eleanor wasn't here. She would have enjoyed it.

"You know," said Vince, as he helped himself to a miniature pumpkin pie and a glass of mulled wine, "you've really got more Indians than you need. You might want to think about culling the collection or at least selling off some of the pieces."

"Collecting is one thing," said Franklin. "Breeding is another."

"So," said Vince, grinning from ear to ear, "what are you going to name the little rascals?"

The next morning, Hudson got up bright and early. The house was warm and still smelled of pine scent, and the bright winter sun flooded the kitchen with light. He hummed as he put the coffee on and buttered a croissant. He'd take some treats down to the camp, though he wondered whether mincemeat would be too sweet for the Indians. And he had decided what to get them for Christmas. A music box. A particularly lovely music box that he had seen at Bates Antiques that played "Oh Come, All Ye Faithful" when you lifted the lid. Inside, porcelain Victorian figures, bundled up in bright red clothes, skated around in a circle on a tiny mirror in time to the music.

Hudson was just finishing wrapping individual clementines in bright paper, when the phone rang.

"Merry Christmas, honey," said Eleanor.

Hudson smiled and walked to the window. "You'll never believe what happened."

"Tell me," said Eleanor. "You know I love surprises."

The sun was burning off the last of the mist in the valley, and, in that moment, Hudson felt his whole body go numb. He blinked. And then he blinked again. The valley was empty. The tipis were gone. And so were the Indians.

"Honey," said Eleanor, "are you still there?" But the only sound she heard was the phone hitting the floor.

When the police arrived, they found Hudson stomping through the valley, shouting and throwing clumps of ferns into the beaver ponds, and rather than upset him any further, the officers quietly retreated to the porch and watched him from there until Eleanor arrived home.

"Stolen," Hudson told Eleanor, after she helped him out of his wet clothes. "Some bastard stole my entire collection."

"Calm down, honey," said Eleanor. "I've already talked to the police, and the good news is that no one has stolen your collection."

"But my Indians are gone!"

"That's right," said Eleanor, patting his hand. "But it looks as though they've wandered off on their own."

"That doesn't make any sense."

"Well, of course it doesn't, and they'll be back."

"You think so?"

"Where would they go?" Eleanor shook her head and smiled. "Besides, you silly goose, they're all insured."

The Indians didn't return, and Hudson had to work at

being cheery when everyone arrived at his house for the Boxing Day party.

"Vince and I drove around the neighbourhood a couple dozen times," Franklin told him, "but nothing's turned up yet."

"About the most you can do now," Vince offered, "is post a reward and hope someone finds them before the weather really turns cold and they all freeze to death."

Just before midnight, Eleanor found Hudson in the kitchen, staring out the window. "Come on, honey," she said, softly, "the new millennium is almost here. Why don't we go in the living room and join our friends."

"Romulus and Remus," said Hudson. "That's what I was going to name them. After the Roman twins."

"Weren't they raised by a wolf?"

Hudson smiled and nodded.

"Such a clever man," said Eleanor, "and so sweet." And she kissed her husband just below his ear. "Tell you what. Why don't we drive over to Kingston next week and visit Jonathan and Cynthia? We could get a reservation at that bed and breakfast you like so much. Cynthia's been dying to show us their collection of African ivories. That'll cheer you up."

Hudson leaned on the window sill and sighed. "We have so much to be thankful for, don't we."

Eleanor snuggled in against him. "Yes, we do."

Outside, the moon was full. Hudson could see the entire valley, laid out under the stars, pristine, silent, and white. Perhaps he'd buy that music box anyway and leave it on one of the stumps near the large beaver pond, just in case the Indians were waiting in the woods.

In the living room, Eleanor, Vince and Franklin and his other friends and neighbours began singing "Auld Lang Syne," and as he listened to the happy voices, Hudson took comfort in the conviction that the new millennium would be as bountiful and joyous as the old one. To be sure, having his collection vanish like that had been devastating, and he hoped with all his heart that Eleanor was right. But if she was wrong and the Indians did not return, he knew that at some point, while he would always remember each piece—especially Romulus and Remus—he would have to put the loss aside and begin again.

The Dog I Wish I Had,
I Would Call It Helen

Jonathan lay in the tub with just his head and butt out of the water and practised his swimming. "I am swimming because I am four now, and, when you are four, you have to know how to swim."

"That's right," said Helen.

"In case a ghost throws you in the lake."

"It's always good to be safe around water."

"Only the ghost wouldn't do it on purpose. Only if she slipped."

"Let's wash your hair now."

"Am I four now?"

"Yes, honey. Yesterday was your birthday."

"But I didn't get my dog."

"Should I use the bunny soap or the squirrel soap?"

"If I had a dog, it would scare the ghosts away."

"The bunny soap smells like strawberries. Here, smell."

"No, no, no. It wouldn't hurt the ghosts. It would just fool them."

"The squirrel soap smells nice, too. Why, I think it smells like lemons. You like lemons."

"The ghosts would think it was only a pretend dog, and, when they got close, it would jump up and scare them."

"Let's use the squirrel soap this time."

"But I don't have a dog." And Jonathan sat up with a splash and began to cry.

Jonathan stood at the edge of the table and watched the side of his cereal bowl. He stood on one foot, and then he stood on the other.

"Look, Mummy!"

Helen smiled at the book she was reading.

"Look, Mummy!"

"That's nice, honey," said Helen, and she shifted in the chair without taking her eyes off the book.

Jonathan went into the kitchen and dragged his stool back to the table. He climbed on the stool, leaned across the book Helen was reading, took her face in his hands, and turned her head toward him so he could see her eyes.

"You have to look, Mummy."

"You haven't eaten any cereal."

"You have to feed me."

"There are some nice peaches in your cereal."

"You put in the wrong cereal."

"I'll bet you could find those peaches if you looked."

"I don't want peaches. I want you to look."

"I am looking. And you know what I see?"

"A dog?"

"I see some yummy raisins."

"A dog would eat that cereal," said Jonathan. "If I had a dog, it would eat all that cereal."

"Maybe there's a four-year-old who would eat that cereal."

"No, there isn't," said Jonathan, and he dragged the stool into the bedroom closet and shut the door behind him.

That evening, Helen got a cup of water from the bathroom tap. Jonathan was standing on his bed. He had taken off his sleepers, again. His diaper was balanced on his head. Helen held out the cup.

"I don't want that," said Jonathan.

"You said you were thirsty."

"No, I said . . . I said . . . I said I was werstry."

"Oh."

"That's how dogs talk."

"Which story would you like tonight?"

"If I had a dog, I could talk to it."

"Shall we read the one about the donkey?"

"If I had a dog, I wouldn't need you."

"Maybe we should read one of the new books we got from the library."

"My dog could wash my hair and make my cereal."

Helen smiled and gathered Jonathan up in her arms. And before she could catch herself she said, "Maybe we should read the one about the Pokey Puppy."

She felt Jonathan stiffen in her lap, and, almost as

soon as the crying began, she could feel his warm tears pass through her skirt and trickle down her belly.

Helen had read an article on mothers that suggested that you didn't have to be the perfect mother. In fact, it said that mothers who did everything might actually be injuring their children by removing all the frustrations and obstacles from their lives, things that tended to educate and strengthen. What one should strive for, the article said, was to be a "good-enough mother," someone who loved her children but who didn't try to protect them from all of life's difficulties.

Jonathan's father was in San Francisco, and when Helen called him one night to see how he was doing, she told him about the good-enough mother. "Honey," he said, "you're one hell of a lot better than just good enough." Which was not what Helen had wanted him to say.

"What I mean," she said, "is that you can't do everything for children. They need to grow and learn and sometimes that's hard." And then she confessed that she hadn't bought Jonathan a dog.

"I thought you were going to get him a dog."

"I was, but I think it would just be too much work."

"It would give him something to look after."

"It would give me something else to look after."

"I'm sorry, honey."

"It's not your fault."

"You know what I mean."

Helen stood up and moved quickly to the bathroom. Long-distance phone calls brought on bowel movements. Helen didn't know why, and she had never heard of anyone who had a similar problem, though, in truth, she hadn't asked around. The phone would ring; she would answer it and hear that long-distance hollowness, and, before the person on the other end said anything, Helen would feel the sensation of things on the move. If the conversation was short, she found she could tighten her muscles and endure, but until she bought the portable phone, longer conversations were always broken with intermissions.

"Are you coming up at Christmas?"

"Is that okay with you?"

It was not a problem so much as a puzzle. At one point, she decided it wasn't the phone call itself but the person calling. Her mother calling from Prince Edward Island. Sam calling from San Francisco. Local calls didn't affect her at all. But then, one day, Canadian Airlines called to correct an error in a ticket she had booked, and she couldn't get to the bathroom fast enough. She had heard of people experiencing this problem in bookstores and large libraries. It had something to do with the chemicals that were used to make paper.

"Jonathan would like to see you."

"How about you?"

Helen could see the edge of the shower curtain. It was picking up mildew and grey stains along the bottom. The toilet paper dispenser was almost empty.

"It would be nice to see you."

"I'm sorry."

"It really would be nice to see you."

After they hung up, Helen was sorry she had said it in exactly that way. She should have set up a few more barriers, so that there was some effort involved. Sam would have the wrong idea now. He would think she was lonely, desperately lonely, perhaps, when she wasn't. He would think that she missed him, and, while she did, in a modest way, she only missed him sometimes late at night and occasionally on the weekends, when her law office was closed and she had time to think about anything.

She should have said, "Let me know what you want to do." No, that wasn't it, either. She wished she had xeroxed a copy of the article.

When she picked up Jonathan from the daycare on Monday, he gave her a heart he had cut out himself. All around the edges were patches of glue and glitter. There was a piece of yarn strung through the top of the heart and tied in a loop. In the centre was a series of colourful scribbles that took on a vague form. At the bottom of the heart, one of the daycare workers had written, "I love you, Mummy."

"This is lovely, honey. Is it for me?"

"Yes," said Jonathan.

"Do I hang it around my neck?"

"Yes, that is what the string is for. You hang it around your neck because it is your heart."

"Is this a picture of me?" And Helen pointed to the lines and swirls at the centre of the piece of red cardboard. "No," said Jonathan. "That is the dog I wish I had." That evening, after supper, Jonathan brought out the quilted pad from his crib and a table knife from the kitchen.

"We have to play the game," he said.

About a year ago, Jonathan had crawled into bed with Helen, curled up against her stomach, and told her to push so he could be born. She pushed, and Jonathan was born morning after morning. At first, she was delighted with his interest in birth and his understanding of the process, which included, not without emotional difficulties, Caesarean section. Some days Jonathan would be born vaginally, and some days Jonathan would have to cut her open so he could escape. On the days when a section was called for, he would run his finger over her scar and ask her if it still hurt. Later, the game became more elaborate with Helen having to walk the floor in an attempt to turn the baby so it could be born naturally.

The morning game was a nice game because Helen was still half-asleep and didn't have to do much, but as the game progressed and gathered more elaborate rituals and equipment, it also became a burden. She had invited George and Mary and Sid and Elizabeth over for drinks one night, and Jonathan had come into the living room dragging a blanket and a table knife. Helen had laughed and explained the game, hoping honesty would quell the embarrassment. They all said what a clever boy

Jonathan was and what an imagination! Then they fell into a conversation about what babies really knew and how they were probably much more aware of what was happening than parents gave them credit for. The whole time they talked, Jonathan tried getting his head under Helen's skirt and later settled for lying across her lap and twiddling with her nipples.

The pad from the crib was the newest piece of equipment. There were elastic straps on each corner of the pad and Jonathan would have Helen put both her arms though the top straps and her legs through the bottom straps so the pad functioned as a cotton womb into which Jonathan could crawl and be pushed out. The elastic straps were not very comfortable, and, in spite of her interest in Jonathan's imagination, Helen, of late, had begun to find the game tedious.

"Mummy's a little tired tonight, honey. Maybe we could play that game another time."

"No. I have to be born."

"Maybe we could put the pad on the floor and you could crawl under it and you could be born that way."

"No. That is not the way babies are born. I am a baby."

"Well, little baby, maybe you could crawl under one of the cushions and be born that way."

Jonathan curled his lip and lowered his forehead. "Babies are not born that way. They have to come out the 'gina, and the doctor cuts them out with a knife. Did they cut me out with a knife?"

"Yes, honey."

"Did it hurt me?"

"No, I don't think so."

"Did it hurt you?"

"Just a little."

Actually, Helen recalled, it had hurt a lot. When she came out of the anaesthetic, the first sensation she felt was nausea. The second sensation was pain, as if she had been cut in half. She lifted the covers and could just see the tops of the thick staples holding her groin together. They reminded her of the staples she had seen her father use to nail barbed wire to fence posts. When she tried to move, the pain roared up through her body, and she was only just able to turn her head to one side before she threw up.

"Did the doctor use a laser?"

"No, honey."

"He used a knife, right?"

"That's right."

"I think we will have to use a knife this time, too."

Jonathan brought home three cardboard birds and a bag of twigs and spent the evening piling the twigs on top of each other. "This is an ostrich nest," he said. "And this is a baby ostrich and the mother ostrich."

That left one bird. It lay on its side on the floor. Jonathan bounced the other two birds about on the pile of twigs. "They are kissing, Mummy, because they love each other."

"That's nice, honey."

"I love you, Mummy."

"And I love you, my baby ostrich."

"No, no," said Jonathan. "I am a baby lion."

"Are you a hungry baby lion? Should we eat some supper?"

"Yes, I am very hungry."

"What should we eat, baby lion?

Jonathan picked the third bird off the floor. "Ostriches," he said.

The dog had been Sam's idea. He said it would be good for Jonathan to have a pet. Then he said she should get one for companionship. Six months later, Sam was pushing a German shepherd for protection. Finally, he confessed that it was guilt, that he wanted her to be happy and safe.

"I'm fine, Sam. I don't need a dog."

"I know."

"I don't have time to look after a dog."

"I know."

"Jonathan's fine, too."

"Does he miss me?"

"You're his father."

"I've got no excuses."

"We're both fine."

"I'm sorry."

Helen quite enjoyed the graveyard. On her early morning runs, she would wind her way past the markers, trying to read them as she went. She was especially moved by the turn-of-the-century granite angels and women in flowing robes who leaned over the graves casting long shadows on the grass and by the stone crosses that had little oval pictures of the deceased. Sometimes there were Grecian vases and turned pillars or a pair of clasped hands rising out of the rock. The newer gravestones were generally plainer, rectangles and squares, with short, pithy inscriptions, "Beloved Husband," "Together at Last," "Our Mother." There was an entire row of granite slabs set in the ground on the same level as the grass that all said "R.I.P." and then gave the name and the dates.

Helen was most taken with the older graves of children and babies, where stone angels and granite lambs were the rule, and where the inscriptions were great romances: "I Will Lend You for a Short While a Child of Mine, He Said," "Sleep, Sweet Babe, and Take Thy Rest. God Called Thee Home; He Thought It Best." There was a large stone with a harp carved on its face that said, "Gone to Be an Angel." Right next to it was an oval stone that simply said, "Ashes and Dust, Angelina, Dead at Birth."

Helen's favourite was a small stone with a figure in a robe holding a lamb. It was the grave of a young girl who had died of cholera at the age of three. "Budded on Earth to Bloom in Heaven" was carved at the base. It was the halfway point on her run, and she always paused a moment to read the inscription. Some days she would shake her head and laugh; other days she would cry. And then she would turn around and run home.

One Saturday, Helen took Jonathan to the graveyard. There was a large, yellow backhoe at the far end of the cemetery and a small group of people standing around a pile of dirt.

"Look, Mummy, a tractor!"

"It's a backhoe, honey. They're burying someone who died."

"They are putting a dead person in a hole, right?"

"That's right."

"Because they died?"

"Yes."

"Is Daddy dead?"

"No, Daddy is in San Francisco."

"When he dies, will they bring him back and put him in a hole?'

"They have graveyards in San Francisco, too."

Helen took Jonathan by the grave with the woman and the lamb. "This little girl's name was Amy. She was only three when she died."

"She was never four?"

"No, she died before she was four."

"Are you going to die, Mummy?"

The stone lamb had had one of its legs knocked off and there was a chip out of the woman's shoulder.

"Yes, I'm afraid so. Some day."

"Yeah," said Jonathan, "me too."

Jonathan talked about the graveyard for a week and concluded that Amy got sick and died because her father had gone to San Francisco and was gone too long, and her mother didn't hear her crying because her mother was running home but didn't get there in time because she kept falling in holes.

Helen took inordinate pride in Jonathan's imagination. Nevertheless, she stopped running in the mornings and began playing squash during her lunch break.

Sam called in early December to say he couldn't make it up. He wanted to know if she had thought any more about a dog, and Helen told him that she had decided not to get one.

"How does Jonathan feel about that?"

"It would be better if you didn't mention it to him."

"I'd really like to get him one."

"I know."

"What should I get him for Christmas, then?"

On Christmas Eve, Jonathan lay in the tub and declared that he no longer wanted a dog.

"What would you like for Christmas?"

"Daddy."

"Daddy can't come."

"Then I don't want anything."

Helen rubbed Jonathan's back and pushed the warm water up on his neck. "Maybe you'd like a tricycle."

"No, I don't want a tricycle."

"Maybe you'd like some books."

"No. I want you to hold me."

"Do you want me to hold you now?"

"Yes. I want you to hold me for eighty-two minutes."

"That's a long time."

"Did the little girl's mother hold her for eighty-two minutes?"

After Jonathan went to sleep, Helen made herself some tea and cinnamon toast and sat in the straight-back chair and watched the night turn blue-black and moonless in the kitchen window.

The Baby in the Airmail Box

Okay, so on Monday

The baby arrives in a cardboard box with a handful of airmail stamps stuck on top and a label that says, "Rocky Creek First Nations."

Orena Charging Woman brings the box to the council meeting and sets it in the middle of the table. "All right," she says, after all of the band councillors have settled in their chairs, "who ordered the baby?"

"Baby?" says Louis Standing, who is currently the chief and gets to sit in the big chair by the window. "What baby?"

Orena opens the airmail box and bends the flaps back so everyone can get a good look.

"It's a baby, all right," says Jimmy Tucker. "But it looks sick."

"It's not sick," says Orena, who knows something about babies. "It's White."

"White?" says Louis. "Who in hell would order a White baby?"

And just then

Linda Blackenship walks into Bob Wakutz's office at the Alberta Child Placement Agency with a large folder and an annoyed expression on her face that reminds Bob of the various promises he has made Linda about leaving his wife.

"We have a problem," says Linda, who says this a lot, and she holds the folder out at shoulder level and drops it on Bob's desk. Right on top of the colour brochure for the new Ford trucks.

"A problem?" says Bob, which is what he says every day when Linda comes into his office and drops folders on his desk.

"Mr. and Mrs. Cardinal," says Linda.

When they were in bed together, Bob could always tell when Linda was joking, but now that they've stopped seeing each other (which is the phrase Bob prefers) or since they stopped screwing (which Linda says is more honest) he can't.

"Have they been approved?"

"Yes," says Linda.

"Okay," says Bob, in a jocular sort of way, in case Linda is joking. "What's the problem?"

"They're Indian," says Linda.

Bob pushed the truck brochure to one side and opens the file. "East?"

"West."

"Caribbean?"

"Cree."

"That's the problem?" says Bob, who can't remember if giving babies to Indians is part of the mandate of the Alberta Child Placement Agency, though he is reasonably sure, without actually looking at the regulations, that there is no explicit prohibition against it.

Linda stands in front of Bob's desk and puts her hands on her hips. "They would like a baby," she says, without even a hint of a smile. "Mr. and Mrs. Cardinal would like a White baby."

Meanwhile

Orena takes the baby out of the airmail box and passes it around so all the councillors can get a good look at it.

"It's White, all right," says Clarence Scout. "Jesus, but they can be ugly."

"They never have any hair," says Elaine Sweetwater. "Got to be a mother to love a bald baby."

Now, the baby in the airmail box isn't on the agenda, and Louis can see that if he doesn't get the meeting moving, he is going to miss his tee time at Wolf Creek, so when the baby is passed to him, he passes it directly to Orena and makes an executive decision.

"Send it back," he says.

"Not the way it works," says Emmett Black Rabbit. "First you got to make a motion. Then someone has to second it."

"Who's going to bingo tonight?" says Ross Heavy Runner. "I could use a ride."

"Maybe it's one of those free samples," says Narcisse Good. "My wife gets them all the time."

"Any chance of getting a doughnut and a cup of coffee?" says Thelma Gladstone. "I didn't get breakfast."

"We can't send it back," says Orena, "There's no return address."

"Invoice?" asks Louis.

"Nope," says Orena.

"All right," says Louis, who is not happy with the start of his day, "who wants a baby?"

"Got four of my own," says Bruce Carving.

"Three here," says Harmon Setauket.

"Eight," says Ross Heavy Runner, and he holds up nine fingers by mistake.

"You caught up on those child support payments yet?" Edna Hunt asks him.

"Coffee and doughnuts?" says Thelma, "Could we have some coffee and doughnuts?"

"Could someone come up with an idea?" Louis checks his watch.

"What about bingo?" says Ross.

"Perfect," says Louis. "Meeting adjourned."

At the same time

Bob Wakutz is shaking hands with Mr. and Mrs.

Cardinal. "Would you like some coffee?" he says. "Maybe a doughnut?"

"Sure," says Mr. Cardinal. "Black, no sugar."

"Thank you," says Mrs. Cardinal. "One cream, no sugar."

Bob smiles at Linda.

Linda smiles back.

"Maybe we should get down to business first," says Bob, and he opens the file. "I see you've been approved for adoption."

"That's right," says Mrs. Cardinal.

"So, when can we expect to get a baby?" says Mr. Cardinal.

Bob looks at Linda. He still finds her attractive, and, if he's being honest with himself, he has to admit that he misses their get-togethers. "Don't we have several Red babies ready for immediate placement?"

"Yes, we do," says Linda, who has no idea what she saw in Bob.

"Perfect," says Bob.

"That's nice," says Mr. Cardinal, "but we don't want a Red baby."

"No," says Mrs. Cardinal, "what we want is a White baby."

"That's understandable," says Bob. "White babies are very popular."

Indeed

"White babies are very popular," says Louis.

"That's a dumb idea," says Orena, who has heard plenty of dumb ideas in her life, mostly from men.

"Everybody comes to bingo, don't they," says Louis, who has heard plenty of dumb ideas in his life, too, mostly from politicians.

"You can't give the baby away as a bingo prize."

"Why not?"

"Nobody wants to win a baby," says Orena. "Babies are a dime a dozen."

"This isn't just any baby," says Louis, who knows this is the best idea he is going to come up with. "This is a White baby. You make up the posters. I'll call the newspapers."

While

Bob has to get the coffee and the doughnuts himself. Black with no sugar and one cream with no sugar.

"We try to match our babies with our families," says Bob. He folds his hands in front of his face so he can smell his fingertips. "I think you can see why."

"Sure," says Mrs. Cardinal. "But lots of White people have been adopting Red babies."

"Yes," says Mr. Cardinal. "You see Black babies with White parents, too."

"And Yellow babies with White parents," says Mrs. Cardinal.

"Don't forget Brown babies with White parents," says Mr. Cardinal.

"That's true," says Bob, who is trying to remember

why his left index finger smells the way it does. "And my administrative assistant Ms. Blackenship can tell you why."

"Sure," says Linda, who is particularly grumpy today and who has never liked the thing that Bob does with his fingers. "It's because we're racist."

Which explains why

Louis is late for his golf game and has to drive the golf cart to the third hole at speeds well above the posted limit. He arrives just as Del Weasel Fat hooks his drive into the trees.

"Where the hell you been?" says Vernon Miller, who tells people his handicap is eighteen when it's really ten.

"Council meeting," says Louis. "Usual game?"

"Dollar a hole," says Moses Thorpe. "Greenies, sandies, and snakes. What's in the box?"

"Baby," says Louis, and he grabs his driver.

"Baby what?" says Del, who is thinking about using one of his three mulligans on this hole.

"Baby baby," says Louis. "Everybody hit?"

Moses looks in the box. "Jesus, it is a baby. But it's White."

So everyone has to have a look, and Louis can't hit until everyone is finished looking.

"This one of yours?" asks Vernon.

"Of course not," says Louis. "It came in the mail."

"Are we going to play golf, or what?" says Del, who

has decided against taking a mulligan so early in the round.

Louis hits his drive straight down the fairway. He hits the green with his second shot. And then, with everyone looking, he sinks a thirty-five-foot putt for a birdie. By the time they finish the front nine, Louis is up seven dollars.

"Jesus," says Vernon, "damn thing must be a rabbit's foot."

"Hope you plan to feed it," says Del. "Cause I don't want it crying on the back nine."

"You know what White babies eat?" says Moses, trying to remember a really good joke he heard last week.

"Put on a few more pounds," Vernon tells Louis, "and you'll be able to nurse it yourself."

Everybody has a good laugh, even Moses who can't remember the rest of the joke.

"Come out to bingo tonight," says Louis, holding up seven fingers just to remind everyone how well he's playing. "Maybe you'll get lucky."

But

"We're not racist," says Bob. "It's simply a matter of policy."

"So, race isn't a consideration?" asks Mr. Cardinal.

"Absolutely not," says Bob. "We're not allowed to discriminate on the basis of race, religion, or sexual orientation."

"So," says Mrs. Cardinal, "how do you discriminate?"

"Economics and education," says Bob.

"Well," says Mr. Cardinal, "we're rich."

"Great," says Bob. "We're always looking for rich parents."

"And we're well educated," says Mrs. Cardinal. "Mr. Cardinal has a master's in business administration and I have a doctorate in psychology."

"Terrific," says Bob. "I'm a college graduate, too."

"We love children," says Mrs. Cardinal. "But we also want to make a contribution."

"To society," says Mr. Cardinal. "White people have been raising our babies for years. We figure it's about time we got in there and helped them with theirs."

"Admirable," says Bob.

"Both of us speak Cree," says Mrs. Cardinal. "Mr. Cardinal sings on a drum, and I belong to the women's society on the reserve, and we know many of the old stories about living in harmony with nature, so we have a great deal we can give a White baby."

Bob chats with the Cardinals, who reassure him that they would make sure that a White baby would also have ample opportunities to participate in White culture.

"We'd sign up for cable," Mr. Cardinal tells Bob.

"Spectacular," says Bob, and he assures the Cardinals that their case is his number-one priority. "Call me in a week."

After the Cardinals have gone, Linda comes into the office with a fax and drops it on Bob's desk from shoulder level. "There's a big bingo game on the reserve this weekend."

"Fabulous," says Bob, who is running out of adjectives and who is sorry that Linda has started dropping things from shoulder level instead of bending over the way she used to when she wanted him to look at her breasts.

"One of the prizes," says Linda, "is a White baby."

So

When Louis gets to the bingo hall that night with the baby in the airmail box, there's not a single seat left. "I told you this was a good idea," he tells Orena.

"They came for the truck."

"Isn't the truck next week?"

"No," say Orena, "the truck is this week."

"So we have a truck and a White baby tonight."

"Technically," say Orena, "that's correct."

"Okay, so we double up and put the baby with the truck," say Louis, who is pleased to have come up with this without even thinking.

Orena is about to tell Louis that this is another one of his bad ideas, when she sees Bob Wakutz and his administrative assistant, Linda Blackenship, come into the bingo hall.

"Did I tell you I shot an eighty-one today," says Louis. "Maybe you should give *The Herald* a call."

"Forget golf," says Orena. "We've got a problem."

Yes

"We've got a problem," Linda tells Bob. "If you move this way a little and look to the right of the stage, you'll see a heavy-set Indian guy in a gold golf shirt standing next to an Indian woman in jeans and a white top, who is, if I'm not mistaken, related to that Indian woman from Red Deer whose baby we apprehended last month and are in the process of putting up for adoption."

Bob has never been fond of long, compound/complex sentences, but he does support the use of neutral terms such as "apprehended" and non-emotional phrases such as "in the process of putting up for adoption." However, he does not like problems.

"Claimed we had the wrong family," says Linda. "How many times have we heard that one?"

"Hey, look," says Bob. "The grand prize is a new Ford truck."

"What about the baby?" says Linda.

"We'll apprehend it right after the game for the truck," says Bob, and he puts the warrant back in his pocket, stops one of the bingo girls, and buys four cards.

While

Orena and Louis stand by the truck with the baby in the airmail box.

"Those are the two assholes from the Alberta Child Placement Agency who took my cousin's little boy," says Orena. "They must be here for the White baby."

"Problem solved," says Louis.

"You can't give them the baby," says Orena.

"Why not?" says Louis.

"Precedence," say Orena. "We can't let government agencies kidnap a member of the tribe."

"The baby's a member of our tribe?"

"That's probably why it was sent to us," says Orena.

"It doesn't look Indian," says Louis, even though he knows that not all Indian babies look Indian.

"Maybe it's part Indian," says Orena.

"Just great," says Louis. "Things were certainly easier when we were in harmony with nature."

And then

Linda turns to Bob and says, "What if I were to tell you that that baby was ours."

Bob knows that there is a right answer to this question, but he can't remember what it is.

"The White baby?"

"Yes."

"You're kidding," he says, and he's pretty sure that this is not the right answer.

"What if I were to tell you that you got me pregnant," says Linda, "and that, after I gave birth, I mailed it to the reserve in order to punish you?"

Bob puts his fingers in his nose and takes a deep breath. "Our child?"

"What would you say?"

"Wonderful," says Bob, who hasn't run out of

adjectives after all. "Look, there's the truck you can win. God, is it gorgeous!"

"Yes," said Linda. "That's exactly what I thought you would say."

And just then

The game begins. Louis hands the baby in the airmail box to Orena and goes to the microphone to drum up business.

"All right," he says. "Here's the game you've been waiting for. Blackout bingo. First prize is . . . a brand new Ford pickup and a White baby. Any questions?"

Martha Red Horse holds up her hand. "Is there a cash equivalent for the baby?"

"Good luck," says Louis, and he signals Bernie Strauss to start the game before someone else can ask a question.

Linda nudges Bob. "We better do something."

"Linda," says Bob, and he says this in a fatherly way without the hint of reprimand, "look around."

"What's that supposed to mean?" says Linda.

"We're surrounded by Indians."

And with that

Bob sits down next to Mr. and Mrs. Cardinal, who have twenty bingo cards spread out between them.

"Hello," says Mr. Cardinal. "I'll bet you came for that new Ford pickup."

"Hi," says Bob, trying to sound nonchalant. "You here for the truck, too?"

"No," says Mrs. Cardinal.

Bob taps Linda on the hip, though it's more of a pat than a tap. "Look who's here."

"Wish us luck," says Mrs. Cardinal.

And quick as you please

Bernie Strauss begins calling numbers. At first Bob doesn't get any, but then he hits a run of numbers, and before he knows it, he has only two left. Three of Mr. and Mrs. Cardinal's cards also have two numbers left and one of their cards has only one number left. And then one of Bob's numbers is called and he has only one to go.

Even Linda is getting excited.

Okay

"Okay," Louis says to Orena, as he watches the number come up on the big board, "what's the worst that can happen?"

This is a question that Louis asks all the time. This is the question that Louis asks when he hasn't a clue how bad things can get. And this time, he asks it just as a squad of RCMP comes storming into the hall.

"Oh, great," says Orena. "Now you've done it."

"B-8," Bernie shouts.

"Bingo!" shouts Bob, and he leaps out of his chair. "Bingo, bingo, bingo!"

And then

The RCMP confiscate the new Ford pickup.

"You don't have a permit," the RCMP tells Louis. "If you don't have a permit, this is an illegal gambling activity."

"It's my truck," says Bob, holding up his card. "See, I have a bingo."

"We have a permit," Louis tells the RCMP, but when he turns to find Orena to ask her to show the RCMP the permit, he finds that she is gone.

"We also heard that you were giving away a White baby," says the RCMP.

"I suppose we need a permit for that, too," says Louis.

"What about my truck?" says Bob. "What about my truck?"

Well, then

Two weeks after the raid on the bingo game, Orena's cousin calls to thank her for the White baby. "Where in the world did you get it?"

"In the mail."

"And they say *we* don't know how to look after our kids."

"You can keep it if you want," Orena tells her cousin.

"We've filed a suit against the Alberta Child Placement Agency," says Orena's cousin. "The idiots had me mixed up with a woman in Medicine Hat. Should have my son back by the weekend."

"So, you don't want the White baby?" says Orena.

"Come on, cuz," says Orena's cousin. "You know any skins who want a White baby?"

"It's tough," says Orena. "They just aren't that appealing."

"I suppose you can get used to them," says Orena's cousin. "What do you want me to do with it?"

"Drop it in the mail," says Orena. "I'll figure out something."

In the meantime

Bob gets out of jail, while the Crown reviews the case. "Can you believe it," he tells Linda. "They take my truck, and they arrest me."

"You hit an RCMP officer."

"I didn't hit him," says Bob. "I stumbled into him by mistake."

"Is that what you tell your wife?" says Linda, who is not ready to let bygones be bygones.

"I'm going to leave her," says Bob, who finds that he is sexually aroused by Linda's reluctance and condemnation. "You just have to be patient."

"And what about that White baby?"

"What about my truck?" says Bob. "The White baby thing was probably just a gimmick to get people to come to bingo."

Okay, so on Monday

Coyote and the Enemy Aliens

You know, everyone likes a good story. Yes, that's true. My friend Napioa comes by my place. My good place. My good place by the river. Sometimes that Napioa comes by my good place and says, tell us a good story. So I do. Sometimes I tell those good stories from the Indian time. And sometimes I tell those good stories from the European time. Grown-up stories. Baby stories.

Sometimes I take a nap.

Sometimes I tell Coyote stories. Boy, you got to be careful with those Coyote stories. When I tell those Coyote stories, you got to stay awake. You got to keep those toes under that chair. I can tell you that.

You better do that now. Those toes. No, later is no good.

Okay, so I'm going to tell you a Coyote story. Maybe you hear that story before. Maybe not.

Coyote was going west. That's how I like to start that story. Coyote story. Coyote was going west, and when he gets to my place, he stops. My good place. By the river.

That was in European time . . . 1940. Maybe it was 1944. No, it was 1942.

Coyote comes to my house in 1941. Hello, says that Coyote. Maybe you have some tea for me. Maybe you have some food for me. Maybe you have a newspaper for me to read.

Sure, I says. I have all those things.

So Coyote drinks my tea. And that one eats my food. And that one reads my newspaper.

Hooray, says that Coyote. I have found a job in the newspaper.

Maybe you're wondering who would hire Coyote.

I thought so.

Okay, I'll ask.

Who would hire Coyote? I says.

The Whitemen, says Coyote. The Whitemen are looking for a Coyote.

Oh boy. Coyote and Whitemen. That's pretty scary.

It's over on that coast, says Coyote. In that west. That's where my job is.

Good, I says. Then I won't have to move.

But I am so hungry, says Coyote. I don't know if I can get to that coast, unless I get something good to eat.

Okay, I says, I will feed you so you can get to that coast.

And I don't have a good shirt, says Coyote. I really need a good shirt, so the Whitemen will see that I'm a good worker.

Okay, I says, I will give you my good shirt.

Oh, oh, oh, says Coyote, how will I get there? It's a very long ways, and my feet are quite sensitive.

You still got those toes tucked under that chair? You better keep your hands in your pockets too. Just in case Coyote notices you sitting there. And don't make any noise. If that Coyote sees that someone is listening to him, that one will never leave.

Okay, I tell Coyote, I will call Billy Frank. My friend Billy Frank goes to the coast. He drives that pickup to that coast to go on that vacation. Maybe he will take you when he goes on that vacation.

Hooray, says Coyote. Hooray!

So Billy Frank takes Coyote to that coast. And that's the end of the story.

No, I was only fooling. That's not the end of the story. There's more. Stick around. Have some tea. Don't move those toes. Coyote is still around here somewhere.

*   *   *

Ho, ho. So a lot of things happen. All of a sudden, everyone is fighting. Mostly those White people. They like to fight, you know. They fight with each other. And then they fight with those other people. And pretty soon everyone is fighting. Even some of us Indians are fighting.

You're probably thinking that Coyote is fighting, too.

Is that what you were thinking?

It's okay, you can tell me.

So Coyote comes back. I warned you about this. Coyote comes back, and he is driving a pretty good truck.

Yoo-hoo, says Coyote, come and see my pretty good truck.

Yes, I says, that's a pretty good truck, all right. That job you got must be a pretty good job.

Oh, yes, says Coyote, that job is the best job I have ever had.

That pretty good truck that Coyote is driving says "Kogawa Seafood" on the door. Ho, that Coyote. Always looking for something to eat.

Where did you get that pretty good truck? I says.

Coyote stole me, says that pretty good truck.

No, I didn't, says Coyote.

Yes, you did, says that pretty good truck.

Don't talk to that silly truck, Coyote tells me.

What's wrong with talking to trucks? I says. Everybody talks to trucks.

Not anymore, says Coyote, and that one lowers his

eyes so he looks like he is sitting on a secret. Talking to Enemy Alien trucks is against the law.

Enemy Alien trucks? Holy, I says. That sounds serious.

National security, says Coyote. If someone saw you talking to an Enemy Alien truck, I might have to arrest you.

I'm not an Enemy Alien, says that truck.

Yes, you are, says Coyote.

No, I'm not, says that truck.

So Coyote and that pretty good truck says "Kogawa Seafood" on the door argue about Enemy Aliens. They argue about that for a long time. All day. Two days. Three. One week. They keep everyone awake. Nobody on the reserve can sleep. Even the dogs are awake.

Knock it off, those dogs says. You're keeping everyone awake.

I haven't heard of any Enemy Aliens, I tell Coyote.

Oh, says Coyote, they're all over the place. But you don't have to worry. You don't have to run away. You don't have to hide under your bed.

That's good news, I says.

Oh, yes, says Coyote. Now that I'm on the job, the world is a safer place.

No, it's not, says that pretty good truck.

Yes, it is, says Coyote. And those two start arguing again.

I don't know about you but all this arguing is making me dizzy. Maybe we should have some tea. Maybe we should have some dinner. Maybe we should watch that television show where everyone goes to that island, practise their bad manners. Maybe we should go to sleep. You can sleep on the couch.

So when I wake up, that pretty good truck is gone. But Coyote is still here.

Where is your pretty good Enemy Alien truck? I ask Coyote.

Oh, says Coyote, I had to sell that one. That's the law now. All Enemy Alien Property must be confiscated. All Enemy Alien Property must be sold. That's my job. And that Coyote shows me a piece of paper says "Order-in-Council 469."

Boy, I says, that paper has a nice voice.

Order-in-Council 469, says that paper. All hail Order-in-Council 469.

Boy, I says, that paper sounds pretty important.

It is, says Coyote. That paper says that I am the Custodian of Enemy Alien Property.

Coyote is the Custodian of Enemy Alien Property, says that paper. All hail Coyote, Custodian of Enemy Alien Property.

That job sounds pretty important, I says.

It is the most important job in the world, says Coyote.

Is it more important than being truthful? I says.

Oh, yes, says Coyote.

Is it more important than being reliable? I says.

Absolutely, says Coyote.

Is it more important than being fair? I says.

Probably, says Coyote.

Is it more important than being generous? I says.

It certainly is, says Coyote.

Holy, I says, that is one pretty important job, all right. How do you do that pretty important job?

Well, says Coyote, first I find all the Enemy Aliens. Then I confiscate their property. Then I sell their property. Say, you want to buy some Enemy Alien Property?

Enemy Alien Property. Yes, that's what that Coyote said. Sure, I don't mind asking. You keep sitting in that chair. Keep those toes under that chair. And stay awake. You start snoring, and that Coyote is going to hear you for sure.

So I ask Coyote, what kind of Enemy Alien Property do you have for sale?

Oh, says Coyote, I have everything. You want a sewing machine? How about a set of dresser drawers? I have a bunch of radios. Cameras? A refrigerator? Blankets? Tea kettles? A wheelbarrow? A house. Maybe you need an easy chair. I got lots of bicycles. Maybe you need a new car. Maybe you need a fishing boat.

A fishing boat? You have a fishing boat for sale?

Ho, ho, says Coyote, I have more than one. How many would you like?

How many do you have? I says.

Eighteen hundred and four, says Coyote.

That's a lot of fishing boats, I says.

It's a hard job, says Coyote. But someone has to be paid to do it. Maybe you need a pretty good kimono.

No, I says, I don't need a pretty good kimono.

Come on, says Coyote. Let's go see the Enemy Alien Property.

So I go with Coyote. But we don't go in that pretty good truck says "Kogawa Seafood" on the door because Coyote has sold it. But that coyote has another pretty good truck says "Okada General Store" on the door.

You sure have a lot of pretty good trucks, I says.

Oh, yes, says Coyote, I am an excellent Custodian of Enemy Alien Property.

So Coyote starts driving. He drives to those mountains. And that one drives into those valleys. And then he drives to that Pacific National Exhibition in that Vancouver city.

I am lost, I tell Coyote. Where are we now?

Hastings Park, says Coyote.

That Hastings Park is a big place. Big buildings. Big signs. That big sign says "Livestock Building."

Livestock? All right. So I ask Coyote, you got any Enemy Alien Horses? That's what I ask. You got any Enemy Alien Horses? I could use a good Enemy Alien Horse.

That Coyote checks that list of Enemy Alien Property. That one checks it again. No, he says, there are no Enemy Alien Horses.

Enemy Alien Cows? I ask Coyote.

No, says Coyote, no Enemy Alien Cows.

Chickens?

No.

Sheep?

No.

Holy, that's all the livestock I can remember. So I ask that Coyote, what do you keep in that Livestock Building?

Enemy Aliens, says Coyote. That's where we keep the Enemy Aliens.

Boy, that Coyote likes to tell stories. Sometimes he tells stories that smell bad. Sometimes he tells stories that have been stretched. Sometimes he tells stories that bite your toes. Coyote stories.

That's one good Coyote story, I tell Coyote. Enemy Aliens in a Livestock Building.

No, no, says Coyote. This story is not a good Coyote story. This story is a good Canadian story.

Canadian story. Coyote story. Sometimes it's hard to tell the difference. All those words begin with C.

Callous, carnage, catastrophe, chicanery.

Boy, I got to take a breath. There, that's better.

Cold-blooded, complicit, concoct, condemn.

No, we're not done yet.

Condescend, confabulate, confiscate, conflate, connive.

No, not yet.

Conspire, convolute, crazy, crooked, cruel, crush.

Holy, I almost forgot cupidity.

No, no, says Coyote. Those words are the wrong words. The word you're looking for is legal.

Boy, you're right, I tell Coyote. That legal is a good word. You can do a lot with that one. That's one of those magic words. White magic. Legal. Lots of other White magic words.

Patriotic, Good, Private, Freedom, Dignity, Efficient, Profitable, Truth, Security, National, Integrity, Public, Prosperity, Justice, Property.

Sometimes you can put two magic words together. National Security, Public Good, Private Property.

Stop, stop, says Coyote. All these words are giving me a headache. We only need one word for Enemy Aliens. And that one word is legal.

So Coyote takes me into the Livestock Building and that one shows me the Enemy Aliens.

Boy, I says, you caught a big bunch of them.

You bet, says Coyote.

But what is that smell? I ask Coyote.

Pigs and cows and horses, says Coyote. We had to move the pigs and cows and horses out so we could move the Enemy Aliens in.

That is certainly a strong smell, I says.

It certainly is, says Coyote. We better leave before we get sick.

Maybe the Enemy Aliens would like to leave, too, I tell Coyote. So they don't get sick from the pigs and cows and horses used to live here.

Enemy Aliens don't mind that smell, says Coyote. They're not like you and me.

They look like you and me, I says.

Oh, no, says Coyote, you are mistaken. They look like Enemy Aliens.

So that Coyote shows me all those sights. That one shows me that big building with all that glass. And that one shows me that other big building with all that glass. And then that one shows me that other big building with all that glass.

Boy, I tell Coyote, that's a lot of big building with glass.

You want to see another big building with glass? says Coyote.

No, I says, that's enough big buildings with glass for me.

Okay, says Coyote, let's go see that Enemy Alien Property. Maybe we can find you some silverware.

So that Coyote shows me that Enemy Alien Property.

Holy, I tell Coyote. It looks like you confiscated everything.

Yes, says Coyote. The Whitemen have given me a commendation that I can hang on my wall.

Boy, there's another one of those words begins with C.

See anything you like? says Coyote. I can give you a really good deal on family heirlooms.

But just as Coyote is showing me those good deals on those family heirlooms, he gets that phone call. This is before they got those phones you can walk around the house with and this is before those phones you can carry in your pocket. Call any place you like for thirty cents a minute, plus those roaming charges. This is the time when those phones are nailed on those walls, when those real women place that call for you, when you have to stand right next to them.

No, not the real women.

So that Coyote stands next to that phone and that one nods his head and that one smiles and that one makes happy noises.

Good news, says that Coyote. The Whitemen have given me another job.

Boy, I says, you are one busy Coyote.

Yes, says Coyote, and I have a new slogan. You want to hear it?

You want to hear Coyote's new slogan? No, I don't want to hear it either. But if we say, no, we may hurt Coyote's feelings and that one is going to cry and make a lot of noise and keep everyone awake. Yes, that one will keep the dogs awake, too.

*　*　*

So I tell Coyote, Okay, you tell us your new slogan.

Okay, says Coyote. Here it is. "Let our slogan be for British Columbia, 'No Japs from the Rockies to the seas.'"

Ho! That your new slogan?

Ian Alistair Mackenzie, says Coyote. It's Ian Alistair Mackenzie's slogan.

He must be important, I tell Coyote. All Whitemen with three names are important.

He's the Whiteman in charge of making up slogans, says Coyote. But that one is not a good poet. If he was a good poet, he would have said, "Let our slogan for British Columbia be, 'No Japs from the Rockies to the sea.'"

Look at that, I says. Now that slogan rhymes.

Be, sea, says that slogan. Be, sea.

Oh, yes, says Coyote, all good slogans rhyme. You want to hear some of Ian Alistair Mackenzie's other slogans?

Is that your new job? I says. Making those Ian Alistair Mackenzie slogans rhyme?

Oh no, says Coyote, my new job is to Disperse Enemy Aliens.

No, I don't know what "disperse" means. Lots of those words begin with "dis." Disdain, Disappear, Distress, Disaster, Disillusioned, Disappointed, Disingenuous, Distrust.

Disperse.

No, I don't think we should ask Coyote. Okay, but don't blame me if things get messed up.

Come on, says Coyote, we got to get those Enemy Aliens dispersed.

So Coyote gets all the Women Enemy Aliens and the Children Enemy Aliens out of that Livestock Building smells like horses and cows and sheep, and that one gets those Men Enemy Aliens with those targets painted on their backs from that other place, and that Coyote puts all the Enemy Aliens into the back of his pretty good truck that says "Okada General Store" on the door.

It's pretty crowded, I can tell you that.

Okay, says the Coyote, let's start dispersing.

So that Coyote drives that truck into the valley, and then that one drives that truck into those mountains, and then that one drives that truck onto those prairies, and that one doesn't stop driving until he gets to my place.

My good place. My good place by the river.

Holy, I says, there is my good place.

Yes, says Coyote, this is a good place, all right. Maybe this is a good place to disperse the Enemy Aliens.

Sure, I says, we got lots of room.

So Coyote gets all of the Enemy Aliens out of the truck, and I call my friend Napioa and my friend Billy Frank. Ho, I tell my friends, we got guests.

Okay, my friend Napioa and my friend Billy Frank tell me. We'll call the rest of the People. Maybe we'll eat some food. Maybe we'll drink some tea. Maybe we'll sing a welcoming song.

A party? says Coyote. I love parties!

But you know what? Some of those Enemy Aliens look pretty sad. Some of those Enemy Aliens look pretty scared. And some of those Enemy Aliens with the targets on their backs look pretty angry.

Boy, I tell Coyote, those Enemy Aliens don't look too happy.

And after everything I've done for them, says Coyote. And just as that Coyote says this, a big car comes along.

Ho, I says, that is one important-looking car.

Yes, I am, says that important-looking car.

Did you come for the Enemy Alien party? I ask that important-looking car.

No, says that important-looking car, I am looking for Coyote.

Did I get a promotion? says that Coyote. And that one polishes his teeth with his tongue.

Get in, says that important-looking car. We got some secret stuff to talk about.

So Coyote gets in that important-looking car, and I go find the food, and now some of the Enemy Aliens are feeling a little better.

You know, that Billy Frank tells me, this story about the Enemy Aliens have their property taken away by Coyote and the Whitemen and get moved from their homes to someplace else reminds me of another story.

Yes, I tell Billy Frank, me, too.

You remember how that story goes, says Billy Frank.

No, I says, but maybe we think about it, that story will come back.

So we eat some food, and we drink some tea, and Billy Frank and Napioa warm up that drum, and we have a couple of songs.

So pretty soon, that Coyote gets out of that important-looking car. And those RCMPs get out of that important-looking car. And those Politician guys get out of that important-looking car, singing "O Canada." But they don't sing so good.

Holy, says Billy Frank. We're going to have to get more food.

Okay, says Coyote, all the Enemy Aliens back in the truck!

Let's not be hasty, I tell Coyote. The party is just starting.

No time to party with Enemy Aliens, says Coyote. I got a new job.

Another job? Boy, that Coyote is one busy Coyote.

What is your new job? I ask Coyote.

I got to take the Enemy Aliens to their new homes, says Coyote.

They can stay here, I says. We got lots of room.

Oh no, says Coyote, that would be too dangerous. We got to take the Enemy Aliens who look sad and the Enemy Aliens who look scared to that Sugar Beet Farms. We going to give them jobs.

Okay, I says, working on the Sugar Beet Farms is pretty good money.

We're not going to pay them, says Coyote. These

Enemy Aliens have to work for free, so they can show us that they are loyal citizens.

Boy, I tell Billy Frank, those citizenship tests are tough.

What's a citizen? says Billy Frank.

What about those Enemy Aliens with the targets painted on their backs, who look pretty angry?

Oh, says Coyote, those are the dangerous Enemy Aliens. Those dangerous Enemy Aliens are going to Angler, Ontario.

Holy, I says, those Enemy Aliens must be real dangerous to have to go to Ontario. Have any of the Enemy Aliens caused any troubles?

Not yet, says Coyote, but you can't be too careful.

So that Coyote goes to the centre of the party and stands by the drum, and that one holds up his hands.

Okay, says Coyote, all the Enemy Aliens back in the truck.

Maybe they didn't hear me, says Coyote. And this time he says it really loud. All the Enemy Aliens back in the truck!

But nobody gets back in the truck.

Okay, says Coyote, we going to have to do this the hard way. And Coyote and the RCMPs grab Billy Frank.

Enemy Alien, says that Coyote and those RCMPs.

Silly Coyote, I says, that's not an Enemy Alien. That's Billy Frank.

Are you sure? says Coyote. He certainly looks like an Enemy Alien.

I'm Billy Frank, says Billy Frank.

So that Coyote and the RCMPs grab another Enemy Alien.

No, I says, that's not an Enemy Alien, either. That's my friend Napioa.

Nonsense, says Coyote, I know an Enemy Alien when I see one, and Coyote and the RCMPs grab every one they see. Those Politicians stand behind that important looking car singing "O Canada" and waving flags.

Enemy Alien.

No, I says, that's Leroy Jumping Bull's cousin Cecil.

Enemy Alien.

No, I says, that's Martha Redcrow. She's married to Cecil Jumping Bull's nephew, Wilfred.

I wouldn't stand too close to this story if I were you. Coyote and the RCMPs might grab you. Yes, I'd sit in the corner where those ones can't see you.

Enemy Alien.

No, I says, that's Maurice Moses. He's Leroy Jumping Bull's grandson. Leroy's daughter, Celeste, had twins.

Enemy Alien.

No, I says, that's Arnold Standing Horse. He takes those tourists into these mountains to go hunting.

That silly Coyote even grabs me.

Hey, I says, let me go.

Oops, says Coyote, oops.

You got to stop grabbing everybody, I says.

But Coyote and the RCMPs don't do that. And pretty soon that Coyote has that pretty good truck filled with Enemy Aliens, and that one has that pretty good truck filled with Indians.

I have more Enemy Aliens than when I started, says Coyote. I must be better than I thought.

You got to keep the Indians and the Enemy Aliens straight, I tell Coyote. Otherwise you're going to mess up this story.

And just then the RCMPs grab that Coyote.

Enemy Alien.

No, no, says Coyote. I'm Coyote.

Enemy Alien, shout those RCMPs. O Canada, sings those politicians. And everybody drives off in that important-looking car and Coyote's pretty good truck says "Okada General Store" on the door.

And I don't see that Coyote again.

So that Coyote comes by my place. My good place by the river.

Yes, this is still the same story. Yes, that Coyote has been gone awhile, but now that one is coming back. Sure, I know where Coyote and the Indians and the Enemy Aliens go. No, they don't go to Florida to play that golf, wrestle that alligator. No, they don't go on that cruise to those islands, everybody sits in the sun and drinks out of big nuts. No, they don't give those Enemy Aliens them back their Enemy Alien Property either.

Hello, says that Coyote. Maybe you have some tea. Maybe you have some food. Maybe you have a newspaper for me to read.

Sure, I says. Sit down. Where's that pretty good truck says "Okada General Store" on the door?

The Whitemen took my pretty good truck, says Coyote. And they took all my Enemy Alien Property. And they took all my Enemy Aliens.

Holy, I says, those Whitemen like to take everything.

Yes, says Coyote, that's true. And that one drinks my tea. And that one eats my food. And that one reads my newspaper.

Hooray, says that Coyote. I have found another job.

Boy, I says, it is dangerous to read newspapers.

This job is better than the other one, says Coyote.

You going to round up more Enemy Aliens? I says.

No, says Coyote. I'm going to that New Mexico. I'm going to that Los Alamos place in New Mexico, help those Whitemen want to make the world safe for freedom.

Okay, I says, that sounds pretty good. That New Mexico is mostly that desert and those mountains. Nothing much in that Los Alamos place that Coyote can mess up.

*   *   *

Yes, now Coyote is gone. Yes, now those toes are safe. Yes, that's the end of the story. Well, you should have asked Coyote that while he was here. Maybe if you hurry, you can catch him before he gets to that New Mexico.

No, I'm going to stay here. That Coyote will come back. That one always comes back. Somebody's got to be here make sure he doesn't do something foolish.

I can tell you that.

Haida Gwaii

He hit an eagle.

The phone rings. I wake up. An eagle, Steven says. Would you believe it? At Queen and Yonge. Making a right turn.

What time is it?

You're Native, he whispers into the phone. Do something.

I squeeze the pillow against my breasts. There are no eagles in Toronto, I tell him. It's a seagull, they don't mind being hit.

A friend in Alberta once showed me an eagle hung on a fence, its head blown away by a farmer from Fort Macleod who feared the bird might want something he owned. Might swoop down and pick his pocket when his back was turned. Steal his truck. Sleep with his wife. Occupy his home.

The buzzer rings. I stand in front of the door and practise breathing. Steven is in the hall with a brown grocery bag. He waits there, smiling, expecting that I'll ask him to come in. My mouth is thick and sticky. My hair is bent to one side. The stubble on my legs catches at my robe.

What do you want?

Here, he says, it's in the bag, and he slides by me, smoothly, rippling into the room, flooding the apartment as he goes.

Nice place.

There are newspapers on the floor. Dishes in the sink. A pile of dirty clothes near the stove. These days I have little to interest eagles. A few books. My mother's sofa. A television with a built-in VCR. A deaf cat.

I have to see a man about a horse, he says.

The bag is heavy. The bottom is dark and wet. I set it on the table and listen to see if he raises the toilet seat. Or if he lowers it. Or if he washes his hands when he's done.

When we were in love and in Haida Gwaii, we stood on the rocks and watched eagles tumble out of the trees each evening to take fish off the water. This is where Raven put Eagle's body in a tree, I told him, and this is where Sun brought her back to life.

So this is where you were born. Far out.

In this particular memory, Steven runs down the beach, his arms thrown out, his clothes catching the wind.

I'm an eagle! His body dips from side to side, weaving in and out of the water, turning and coming back to me on the fly, like a rock thrown at a wall. You're a fish, he says, and pulls me down onto the sand.

Overhead, the seagulls float and search the foam for food. Further out, dark clouds sit on the water. The sand is heavy and damp. Steven pulls his shirt up over his head and kicks off his shoes. He unbuttons my blouse and tosses it into the air. It hovers above us for a moment like a bird.

The eagles do not follow us. They drift back into the tree. They know trouble when they see it.

Afterwards, we walk to where the land and sea turn north and run out to Rose Spit. It is the westernmost point in Canada, a low promontory of sand and storm-thrown grass. Near the end of the spit is a weather tower, a thin-legged platform caught in a web of guy wires. I climb to the top and watch Steven below me, picking his way through the tangle of driftwood and logs at the water's edge. He stands on top of a dead tree and smiles and waves his arms and shouts at me, but all I can hear is the ocean and the sound of the wind. Perhaps it's an apology. Perhaps it isn't.

Steven flushes the toilet and comes back into the room. I didn't mean to hit it, he says. It just flew in front of the car. There was nothing I could do.

Steven smiles at me. He tilts his head to one side the way he used to tilt his head when he wanted me to kiss him or put my head in his lap or make him a cup of coffee.

You with anyone? he says

I want to clean the apartment. Sweep the floor. Make the bed. Organize the refrigerator.

Wash my hair.

Shave my legs.

Take out the trash.

Steven sits down on the sofa, spreads himself out generously, and, in that moment, I realize that the bag might not contain an eagle at all, that it might be filled with doughnuts. Bagels. Fruit. Chocolate. A peace offering. An intention. Perhaps something more. Perhaps something less.

I thought there might be a ceremony, he says, like the one in the story.

I make coffee. Steven stays on the sofa and watches me as I move from the stove to the refrigerator. You're looking great, he tells me. You lose some weight?

In that memory of Haida Gwaii, there is a car on the beach. Stuck sideways in the sand. A car driven too far. A man stands by the rear wheels, a piece of driftwood in his hand. A woman stands near the hood, her arms wrapped around her body. From my tower, I imagine that they are lovers on their honeymoon. The man from Alberta. The woman from Ontario. Perhaps the trip hasn't gone too well so far. A minor accident in Swift Current. A burst radiator hose in Medicine Hat. An argument in Prince Rupert. And, now, at last, this.

The sky above the car is alive with ravens and gulls. They lie on the wind pretending not to listen. I love you, honey, the ravens chant at the gulls. Lot of good that's going to do now, the gulls sing back.

When we take pictures, we tend to take pictures of resting moments. With scenery. But what we remember are the disasters. These are the memories that bind us. These are the memories we share with friends. Standing on the tower I can see the couple in the distance shaping their memories. The car is a rental. Or it was purchased just before the wedding. Or given to them by parents. They are in love and too young to know anything about sand and water. Too young to know to stay on maintained roads. Too young to know how quickly tides shift.

Don't worry, the ravens shout, I know what I'm doing, and the gulls rise up on the gusts and fall away, laughing.

The man digs powerfully with his stick, clearing the tire and the axle so the car can settle deeper into the sand. The woman had already seen the danger long before they made it this far but realized that, even with the protection that passion provides, she could not hope to slow his enthusiasms. While the man works, the woman opens the trunk. Inside, between the suitcases, are brightly coloured shopping bags with twisted paper handles, each overflowing with presents and souvenirs. She looks through each bag, carefully considering each item, finally leaving everything behind and walking across the rocks and the logs, up to where the grass begins.

I watch the ravens and the gulls. They are delighted. The tide is on its way. They know it won't be long now.

That day at Haida Gwaii, I wait on the tower until

Steven finds me. We lean into the wind and watch the man and the woman and the car. Should we help? I ask. The water has almost surrounded the car now.

No point, says Steven. There's nothing worth saving.

What about us?

Steven raises his arms. He pushes me against the guy wires and buries his face in my hair. I'll save you, he says.

At Queen's Quay, Steven takes the bird out of the bag. It is a sorry sight. The body is crushed. Someone has cut off the head and the feet.

Did you do this?

I haven't been with anyone for a long time, he says. What about you?

It's not an eagle, I say, it's a goose, but I can see Steven knows this already.

I've missed you, he tells me.

I stand by the railing and look out over the lake. The wind off the water is cold and quick. Steven hangs the goose in a thin ornamental tree that grows out of an iron grating and interlocking bricks. The branches are too weak to hold the bird, so he wedges it deep in the crotch of the trunk.

And I'm betting you've missed me.

Steven brings back a wing feather. Something for your war bonnet, he says. And he opens my coat and slides the feather inside my blouse.

We should go, I say.

Don't you want to see if the Sun is going to save Eagle? He herds me along the railing with his hands. I still love you, you know.

You're not an eagle, I tell him.

He presses against me gently, and for a moment, over his shoulder, I can see the sky over Haida Gwaii.

I'm not a fish.

The sun comes up and lights the tree and the goose. Steven moves against me, roughly now, his chest rolling against my breasts, his hands pulling my hips into place. I twist and slip away, leaving him hung on the railing, staring at the lake.

Didn't work, he shouts. And when I turn, I see he is holding the goose by a wing. First light glances off its body, and it swings gently from side to side in the breeze, as if it's working up the strength to fly away.

You're Native, Steven says, smiling now, tilting his head to one side. Do something. And he spins the bird around above his head and flings it into the lake.

I walk back to my apartment and lock the door. I pull the curtains and turn off the lights. Later, I lower myself into the bath and watch the water rise around my body. And when I close my eyes, I see the couple on the beach in Haida Gwaii, the man bent on saving the car and the presents, the woman content to have reached high ground.

Little Bombs

So far as Larry could remember, Janice started hiding the bombs the same week that the Plymouth died. There had been symptoms, of course. A deep, grinding growl. Iridescent pools of oil and gas in the driveway. A thumping knock that telescoped up through the steering wheel and made Janice's hands and arms numb.

It was Janice's car, and, for the eight months that it staggered and sputtered about, Larry was sympathetic. "I don't know what to do, honey. We can't afford a new one, and it doesn't make much sense to throw good money after bad." And he would hold her and pat her head.

The car finally collapsed in the Bay parking lot and had to be towed to Ralph's Shell station on Fairfield. "It's not worth the fixing," Ralph told Larry and Janice. "The engine is shot."

They left the Plymouth at the station and drove home in Larry's Chrevrolet, which ran well, but needed two new tires and a tune-up. Larry stood in the front yard that evening and held Janice, watched the sun set, and looked at the Chrevrolet. He kissed her on the forehead and squeezed her. "What the hell," he said. "Let's buy a new car. Damn, let's get a new one."

So Larry and Janice sold the Plymouth to Ralph, who said he could use it for parts, and bought a brand new Ford from Herb Nash. The car came equipped with a stereo radio and tape deck, automatic windows, reclining bucket seats, spoke wheels, cruise control, and an odometer for those long trips. It was a brilliant green, metallic with tiny gold flakes deep in the paint. From a distance, it looked like a gumdrop.

Herb was giving away certificates for a free dinner at the Brown Jug for anyone who bought a new or used car from him, and he was able to enter their names in the company's contest for a free trip to Disneyland, even though the contest had officially closed last Saturday. "Good customers are important to me," Herb said, and he shook Larry's hand, smiled at Janice, and slid the keys across the table. Larry took the keys to the Ford, fished the keys to the Chevrolet out of his pocket, and dropped them into Janice's hand. "We'll get some retreads next month," he said. "But the tune-up will probably have to wait."

The following Monday, after the football game, as he turned off the twenty-eight-inch remote-control colour television he had bought for Janice at Christmas, Larry found the first bomb. It wasn't a large bomb. In fact, it was a very small bomb, about the size of a grape. It was blue, royal blue to be precise. The bomb had been stuck to the back of the television with a wad of gum. The fuse was grey and about an inch long.

Janice was in the kitchen doing the dishes. "Honey," Larry said, "look what I found on the back of the television."

"Oh, that," said Janice.

"It's a bomb, honey," said Larry. "I don't know how it got there."

Janice turned the pot over and scrubbed the black stain. "I put it there."

"You put it there?"

"I bought it at Sam's. I liked the colour."

"Why would you want to put a bomb on the television?"

"It's not a bomb, sweetheart," said Janice. "It's really just a firecracker. It was a joke. Here . . ." And she took a match from above the stove, lit the fuse, and tossed the blue bomb out the window and into the yard.

"See," said Janice. "Hardly any louder than popcorn."

Larry found the next bomb behind the toilet, stuck to the porcelain with a piece of grey duct tape. He had leaned over to find the December issue of *Penthouse,* and there it was. It was slightly larger than the first bomb, and this one was silver. Janice shook her head when he brought it downstairs.

"I found this in the bathroom."

"Honestly, honey," said Janice. "I can't hide anything from you."

"Are you all right?"

"It was supposed to be a surprise."

"You could have damaged the toilet."

"Don't be silly. Here." Janice opened the window. She let the fuse burn down before she dropped the bomb into the hydrangea bush at the side of the house. "That was a little louder, wasn't it?"

That evening, after he had called Janice to tell her he had to work late, Larry went to Cynthia's and told her about the bombs.

"God, Larry," Cynthia said. "Do you think she's crazy?"

"She says it was just a joke."

Cynthia was wearing a black nightgown with slits at the sides. "Why don't we lie down for a while. You need to relax."

Larry kissed Cynthia and gave her right breast a squeeze. "I'm okay. How about making some popcorn? There's a good movie on at eight."

The third bomb shattered the green plastic garbage can and sprayed Larry with coffee grounds and eggshells.

"Well, how was I to know?" Janice said, picking eggshell out of Larry's hair. "You know you never take out the garbage."

Larry's good grey gabardine slacks were badly stained, and there was a wet, grey lump of what looked to be fish intestine on his right wingtip.

"Are there any more?"

"It's just a hobby, honey. I get bored."

The fourth bomb caught Larry's favourite chair and spun the cushions into a cloud of tiny foam particles.

The fifth took off the head of his driver and three wood. The sixth blew out the door on his locker at the health club and started a small fire in his gym strip.

After Larry put out the fire, he drove home. "Janice," he said, "that was a great little trick. I tell you, when that bomb went off, Arnold almost fainted. And as soon as old Harry saw the flames, well, you know Harry."

Janice put down the potato peeler. "Did you really like it? God, I wish I could have been there."

"I must have laughed myself sick." Larry took Janice in his arms and patted her butt and kissed her on the back of her head several times. "I love you very much," he said.

The seventh bomb ripped out the west wall of the garage, most of which fell on the Yamaha all-terrain vehicle that Larry had bought from Jerry Miller less than eight months ago. After Larry cleaned up all the glass and wood, he called Cynthia on the private phone in his den.

"She's still planting those damn bombs," he said.

"You have to call the police, Larry. Does she know about us?"

"Of course not."

"I don't want to find one of her bombs under my bed."

"Don't be silly. She's mad at me."

"Well, what did you do to make her mad?

"Nothing."

"You must have done something."

"I think she likes blowing up my things."

"What if she thinks I'm one of your things?"

Larry spent the next several days thinking about the problem, and, on Thursday, when he came home, he marched right upstairs and found Janice, who was sorting and folding clothes in the bedroom.

"Janice," he said, "we have to talk. These bombs. They have to stop. I know you're angry with me, but bombs are not the solution."

"Oh, Larry," she said. "You worry too much."

"No," he said. "I think the problem is that you don't love me any more."

"Honey, how can you think that?"

"What I mean is that you don't love me enough." Larry unhitched his pants, and undid his new, navy-blue blazer. "Janice, are you having an affair?"

Janice looked at Larry and started to shake her head. Then she smiled and gave him a playful push in the chest. "Oh, Larry," she said. "I've hurt your feelings, haven't I?" And she laughed. "Look, the bombs were pretty silly. I won't buy any more. I'm sorry."

Later that night, after Larry had brushed his teeth, put on his pajamas, and slid into bed, he could hear her downstairs unloading the dishwasher, laughing.

After work the next evening, Larry called Janice to tell her he'd be late getting home again and not to wait dinner.

"I've got to see a client," he said. "It could be a big deal."

Then he drove directly to Cynthia's apartment. She was waiting for him at the door, wearing a soft, rose nightgown.

"What did you spill on yourself?" she asked, looking at Larry's grey slacks.

"She said she was going to stop planting the bombs."

Cynthia put her arms around Larry's neck. "I'm so glad," she said. "You're all tense, honey. Let's go to bed."

"I was beginning to think she wanted to kill me."

"You'll feel better after we make love."

Larry sat down on the sofa. "I don't think I can make love. I'm still upset." He turned on the television. "Is there anything to eat?"

Janice was just bringing the laundry up from the basement when Larry arrived home. "Honey," she said, "you must be starved. Let me put these things away, and I'll heat up dinner for you."

Larry followed Janice up the stairs and into the bedroom. "You can still see the stain in my pants."

"Well, take them off, and I'll drop them at the cleaners. Give me that jacket, too."

Larry took off his pants and his sports coat, and put on his robe. Janice put her arms around his waist. "That's a beautiful robe. I'm glad you bought it. Nothing feels as nice as silk, and you really look good in it."

Larry looked at himself in the mirror and patted his stomach. "Is there any chicken left?"

Janice picked up Larry's coat and pants. Larry looked at himself again before following her downstairs into the kitchen. Janice put the coat and pants over the back of the chair, and, as she did, a little bomb fell out of the coat pocket. Larry stood there in his maroon robe, stunned. "Janice," he said, "I thought you weren't going to do this anymore." He reached down and picked up the bomb. It was bright pink. "I thought you weren't going to do this ever again."

Janice took the pink bomb from Larry and rolled it over in her hand. She held it up to the light and turned it around and around. There was a box of matches on the ledge above the stove and Janice struck one on the burner and lit the fuse. "This isn't one of mine," she said. And she tucked the bomb down the front of Larry's robe.

Larry was still fumbling with the knot when the bomb slipped through, bounced across the floor, and exploded in front of the sink. A small cloud of dense, grey smoke rose from the floor and rolled out into the hall, where it set off the fire alarm. There were large pieces of pink foil scattered on the kitchen floor and smaller bits stuck between Larry's toes and his ankles and shins.

Cynthia's phone was busy. Larry tried a number of times, but gave up around midnight, and went to sleep in the leather recliner in the living room. The line was still busy the next morning, and Janice was gone. The ringing in Larry's ears went away after a few days. The smell of gunpowder lingered much longer.

The Colour of Walls

Harper Stevenson arrived at work on Friday and discovered that the walls in his office had been painted brown.

"I asked for white," Harper told his secretary, "not brown."

"They're not brown," said his secretary, "they're polar almond."

Harper held his hand up against the wall. "See that?" he said. "Let's paint it again."

On the weekend Harper went to the cottage, played a round of golf at the new resort on the lake, relaxed in the lounge chair on his dock, and arrived at the office on Monday to find his secretary and a tall black woman in yellow overalls and a blue cap waiting for him.

"She'll explain the problem to you," his secretary told him.

The black woman in the yellow overalls and blue cap was considerably taller than Harper, and he had to back up to get the angle right.

"I'm Afua," said the black woman. "I'm the painter."

"There's a problem?"

"No," said Afua, "but you may have to settle for something other than dead white."

Harper walked past the two women straight into his office. If anything, the walls were darker.

"What is going on?"

Afua placed her hands on the walls. "These are old walls," she said. "They have a history. Walls have a memory."

"White," said Harper. "I asked for white."

"I know," said Afua, "but they don't want to co-operate."

Harper sat in the leather chair behind his desk and considered the situation. "Really," he said at last.

"White's a fine colour," said Afua, "but I suspect that this is as white as your walls are willing to go."

The next day Harper brought a can of white paint with him, painted a large white patch on one wall, and watched it as it slowly faded away. He painted the patch again. And again. And again.

"Get the black woman back," Harper told his secretary.

"Actually," said the secretary, "she's Native."

"Native?" said Harper. "She looks black."

"Her father's Native and her mother is from Africa," said the secretary. "And she's part German, too. Just like you."

"Call her anyway," said Harper.

* * *

"So," said Harper, after Afua had walked around the office, "what's this nonsense about the walls?"

"Originally," said Afua, "I think they were darker."

"So the colour is bleeding through?"

Afua stood in the middle of Harper's office and closed her eyes. "The world is full of colour," she said.

"I'm sure that's true," said Harper. "But colours have their place. For instance, black is a fine colour for limousines and evening dresses, while white is the colour of choice for wedding dresses and the walls of offices where important business is conducted."

"How about I paint your office a nice seafoam green?"

"What I need," said Harper, "is white."

"A dark cherry would look quite regal."

"White," said Harper. "I'd like a nice, clean white."

"Old walls," said Afua, "they're great, but if you want bright white you're going to have to move to a newer office or tear out the walls and start over."

The drywalling made a huge mess, and, for most of the time, Harper had to work from his home. But by the end of the week, his walls were a bright white.

"Now isn't this nice?" Harper asked his secretary.

"Oh, yes," said the secretary. "It looks just like cottage cheese. Or teeth."

Harper sat in his office all day, enjoying his new walls, but that evening, when he reached out to turn off the lights, he discovered that his hands had turned black. Not black black, more a dark brown, though perhaps not a true dark brown, but certainly a mid-tone, darker than normal flesh.

When Afua stopped by the next day, Harper stood next to the walls and held out his hands. "You see my problem," he said.

"Not much I can do about that," said Afua. "You're the one who wanted white walls."

"What's wrong with wanting white walls?"

"Nothing." Afua shook her head. "It's just that they're very young," she said. "They don't know much yet. All they know is white."

"And that's what I wanted."

"Then," said Afua, "that's what you have."

"Yes," said Harper, "but what about my hands?"

"Don't hold them up against the wall," said Afua.

It took eight coats of paint and even then Harper wasn't completely happy with the walls or his hands. Some days the walls would be too dark and his hands would look fine, and the next day the walls would look great and his hands would look, well, tawny, which—as Harper recalled from his literature class at university—was one of the polite words for things that were not white.

It was a mystery to be sure, and Harper found that thinking about it made him tired and somewhat cranky. Who would have guessed, he mused to himself, that something as simple as walls could be such a problem.

Bad Men Who Love Jesus

Jesus takes the bus as far as the Rolling Rock Café in Testament, Alberta, and walks the forty miles to the Garden River Indian Reserve.

Hide me, he begs the secretary at the band office, for the love of God, hide me.

You know how to run a copier? Mary hands Jesus the agenda for the band council meeting. Either lend a hand, she tells him, or get out of the way.

Jesus stands at the copier, stacking paper in the cradle and watching the machine collate and staple, collate and staple, collate and staple.

I think I lost them in Medicine Hat, he shouts over the noise. But they could be here any time.

I've put you on the agenda, says Mary, under new business.

I hope it's a luncheon meeting, says Jesus. I'm starved.

* * *

Mary arranges the sandwiches and the soft drinks on the table. No peanut butter and jelly this week, she tells the council. Just tuna.

I hate tuna, says Simon who is called Peter.

Can I have his? says Jesus.

Doesn't look like we have enough, says Andrew, brother of Simon who is called Peter.

Who wants brown bread? says James.

Any pita? says Jesus.

You look familiar, John, brother of James, says to Jesus.

It's Jesus, says Philip. He was just on *America's Most Wanted*.

Holy! says Bartholomew. That must have been exciting.

The council votes to buy a new single-wide for Mary, mother of James and John, whose trailer was destroyed when the propane tank exploded, and approves a request for roof repair from Mary who used to work in the sex trade in Calgary before she returned to the reserve and got her status back.

You sure have a lot of Marys around here, says Jesus.

The council also agrees to grade and oil the lease road and to ask for bids on painting the water tower.

What about me? says Jesus. I've always been a friend to the Indians.

I don't know, says Thomas. What about that "civilizing the savage" business?

Yeah, says Matthew, and all those missionaries.

That wasn't my fault, says Jesus. I didn't tell them to do that.

They used your name, says Thomas.

Everybody uses my name, says Jesus.

Mary opens the door to the meeting room. Martha just called, she says. There are a dozen guys at the Petro-Can in Testament, singing and beating their swords against the side of their van.

See? says Jesus. I wasn't making it up.

Martha says they're headed our way, says Mary.

Great, says Simon the Canaanite who is not called Peter. We've hardly enough food to feed ourselves.

You know, says Judas, I'm getting a little tired of sharing.

This is good tuna, says Jesus. Is there any root beer?

The band council walks to the edge of the reserve and they all watch as the evening light shifts and stretches out across the prairies.

If you move fast, says James, son of Alphaeus, you can be in the mountains in a couple of days.

We'll try to slow them down, says Judas. What'd you say to get them so excited?

If thou wilt be perfect, go and sell that thou hast and give it to the poor, says Jesus. Something like that.

Oh yeah, says Philip, that would do it.

Any of you guys interested in following me? says Jesus. I could make you fishers of men.

Thanks anyway, says Matthew, but it screws up our tax status if we work off-reserve.

It's dark by the time the band council gets back to the town site.

So, what did you think? says Simon who is called Peter. You figure they'll find him?

Lots of wilderness out there, says Bartholomew. He should be safe.

I don't know, says Thomas, looking up at the stars in the heavens. They found him once. Maybe they'll get lucky and find him again.

The Closer You Get to Canada, the More Things Will Eat Your Horses

The Fernhill Senior Game Preserve was alive with activity. All morning, the trucks had been bringing in the racks of camouflage clothing, tins of candle black, and hundreds of pairs of high-top boots, running shoes, and woolen gloves.

Mason Walthers leaned on his cane. The arthritis was getting worse. He could feel it in his knees and hips now. It would be sheer luck if he got through another season.

"Next!" said the blond man in the blue suit. Mason couldn't keep track of them anymore. They all looked alike. There was a silver badge on his blazer: "Henry Culler, Assistant Director of Sport."

Mason shuffled to the counter and handed in his card. The Assistant Director of Sport smiled at Mason and looked at the card. "Mason Walthers, seventy-two, male, six-foot-one-inch, one hundred and sixty pounds."

Mason smiled back. "That's right. I think I get complete camouflage this year."

The Assistant Director of Sport looked at the card

again. "Yes," he said, "that's right, Mr. Walthers. How are the legs?"

"Not what they used to be."

"Do you want boots or shoes?"

"Shoes, I think. The feet swell too much for boots anymore."

"Candle black?"

"Wouldn't be without it."

"Cap and gloves?"

"Are they camouflage, too?"

"The gloves are grey, but there was a foul-up and the only caps we got were the orange ones. I wouldn't recommend them."

"The gloves will be fine."

The Assistant Director of Sport handed Mason a neat pile of clothing. On top was a bright, green circle of plastic with a number on it. "You're number two hundred and fifty-six. We may get you up into the three hundreds yet."

"I'd like that," said Mason.

"Have a good season," said the Assistant Director. "Next!"

Mason took his clothes to his room and put them on the bed. Sarah's picture was on the nightstand. Bob had brought her by for Christmas.

"She's only seven, Dad," his son had said, when they arrived at the preserve. "She doesn't understand. Maybe you could explain it to her."

Well, he had tried.

"It's complicated, honey," he had begun. "It has to do with nature. You see, a long time ago, there were a great many animals. Like the kind you see in your picture books. People used to hunt these animals for food, but, after a while, they just hunted them for sport."

"Well, the animals began dying off. There were many reasons. Pollutants killed quite a few. Diseases killed some, too. But most of the animals were hunted until there just weren't any more."

"Human beings are natural hunters, you see. We didn't mean to kill all the animals. It just happened."

And that was as far as he got. Sarah had closed her eyes and curled up in his arms and told him he was being silly. She wanted him to read her the book with all the pictures of horses. "Grandpa, were all the horses beautiful?"

"Yes, honey," he had said. "They were wonderful to see."

"The horse book is my favourite book."

It was Mason's favourite book, too.

What else was he supposed to say? Mason wasn't sure he could explain it anyway. How would he tell a seven-year-old about human psychology and destructive urges, about the wars that had almost destroyed the race and the competitive killing that had begun when there was nothing left to hunt?

There was a knock on the door. Joe Beretta stuck his head around the corner. "Hey, Mason. Come on. They've posted the times."

When Mason got to the recreation room, everyone

was crowded around the bulletin board. Mrs. Winchester was standing at the back, leaning on her walker.

"Don't think it's going to matter much this year," she said, as Mason came up beside her. "Can't push this contraption through the trees without making one hell of a noise. How's that granddaughter of yours?"

"Saw her at Christmas," said Mason. "She'll be eight in July."

"Hey, Mason!" Joe was waving at him from the front of the crowd. "We got an early start. Six-thirty."

"If you're in our group, Mrs. Winchester, we'll give you a hand to the trees. You can hide the walker in the brush near the ravine."

Mrs. Winchester shook her head. "Myrtle Smith and Liz Wesson tried to help old Howard Luger last year. They actually carried him across the meadow. Never saw the like. Got as far as the third post before some smartass got them both with one shot. Broke Howard's hip, too."

"I remember that. The guy won some kind of prize."

"I'll be okay. A lot of folk don't want to waste their shot on me. Too slow. No sport in that. They'd rather take a crack at you fast boys."

Last year, Mason had watched Wilma Remington hobble across the meadow. She was using two canes, and when she got to the sixth post, she had to stop. She stood there for a long time bent over those canes. Her whole body heaving from the exertion. And then she started walking again. She got as far as the first tree. Someone had waited all that time, had waited until she was almost safe before trying a long and difficult shot.

"Thank God for the kids, Mason. They're the only thing that makes all this worthwhile."

Joe caught up to Mason and pulled him off to one side. "Mason, this is the year. We got to do it this time."

Joe always had grand ideas of escaping and heading for Canada. Canada didn't have a seniors law. There had always been rumours of some families smuggling their parents and grandparents across the line. But they were only rumours.

"Look at us, Mason. We're not going to make it through another season. Your legs are all but gone. My back's so bad I can hardly move. I've run out of places to hide."

Every year since Mason had known him, Joe had talked about escape. One year, he was going to dig under the fence. Another time he was going to climb one of the large trees near the perimeter and swing across. The last few years, he had worked up several plans to hide in a delivery van.

Mason liked Joe, but Joe didn't understand the larger picture. "Joe, even if you did get to Canada, it wouldn't change a thing. People die. It's a natural process. What does it matter if you get run down by a drunk driver or shot by someone having a good time? At least here you're part of a delicate balance that keeps human beings from blowing themselves up. You ought to read your history."

"Something's gone wrong, Mason. Can't you see it? It's all wrong."

"What about your friends, Joe?"

"Most of them are dead. Remember. Every season we watch them get shot."

"What about your family? If I went to Canada, I wouldn't be able to see my granddaughter."

"You won't be able to see her if you're dead, either."

Mason went back to his room and lay on the bed. He had been at Fernhill now for seventeen years and, aside from the six weeks of hunting season each spring, they had been good years. He had his own room with a bath, a remote-control television, books, all his meals prepared. Sarah could visit him whenever Bob had the time to bring her by. He didn't like being shot at any more than Joe did, but that was what happened when you turned fifty-five. That was life.

At four o'clock, Mason was awake. The alarm was set for five o'clock and breakfast wouldn't be for another half an hour after that. But he was awake. The leg was throbbing, and, as he shifted around to get out of bed, the pain increased until he had to stop and catch his breath.

He was going to die. Perhaps today. Certainly before the week was out. He could stay in bed and put it off. But you were only allowed three sick days during the season, and, after that, they carried you out to the first post and left you there. His heart was racing as he swung his legs over the edge, and the pain came back, hard and raw, a grinding, breaking pain that Mason imagined was very much like the pain of a bullet smashing into bone.

Mason showered, stood in the hot, streaming water and the steam, slowly working the leg to life. The hunters would come in through the turnstiles at six o'clock, but they had to walk through three miles of forest before they got to the meadow. Others would take blinds closer to the fence and wait for the seniors to come to them. It was five hundred yards from the first post to the trees, and, with any luck, Mason could make the sanctuary of the woods before the hunters got settled.

The first hundred yards was always the hardest, trying to run, trying to stay low, waiting for the crack of the first shot.

Joe was waiting for him at breakfast. "Mason. I'm going to get out," he said. "I've figured out a way."

"Joe, you've always got a way."

Joe leaned across the table. "We get out the same way the hunters get out."

"It's been tried."

"Sure, Benny Ruger tried it with a hunting pass that wouldn't have fooled a blind man. Tried to walk out wearing regulation clothing. They spotted him coming. No, not that way. Not exactly. Look, the first thing we got to do is spot the blinds. Hell, we're good at that."

It was one of the tricks of staying alive during the season. The first day out, you tried to find as many of the blinds as you could. Those who survived the first day shared the information with one another. Halfway through the season the Director of Sport changed the location of the blinds, and you had to start all over again.

Joe leaned even closer. "Here's what we do. We find

two blinds that are close to the main gate and we kill the hunters."

"What!"

"Listen to me. They're trying to kill us, aren't they? And don't give me that crap about it all being part of some damn system. We kill them. Then we change clothes with them, take their passes, and their rifles. We stay in the blind until six and then just leave with the rest of the hunters."

Mason wanted to laugh. "Just what do we kill them with, Joe? Our bare hands? I can hardly wipe my ass. There are pictures on those passes. What happens when the guard looks at the picture?"

"They're going to shoot us, Mason. Unless we get out of here, they're going to shoot us dead. Use a rock. Use a tree limb. Use your imagination. Christ, probably no one is going to check the picture."

The warning bell sounded. People began moving toward the porch. "Meet you back here at six," said Joe.

The meadow was beautiful this time of year, a huge mosaic of greens. Even the posts that marked the distances for the hunters were nicely painted. Later, the flowers would come. Mason especially liked the Ruby Hearts, a tiny, bright-red perennial that appeared suddenly in splashes and pools in the tall grass.

The Director of Sport stood on the platform and looked at his watch. "First group," he shouted. "Go!"

Mason limped down the steps into the grass, willing the leg to move. The trees seemed miles away, and, as he ran, the sweat beaded up on his face and tumbled into his eyes, blinding him. But he kept running, feeling the ground as he went, staying as low and inconspicuous as his tortured body would let him.

Joe found him at dinner. "I've got two blinds near the gate. Couple of old guys. Another year or two and they'll be in here instead of out there."

"I don't know, Joe. Couldn't we just knock them out?"

Joe shook his head. "Mason, we're killers. Man's a killer. How do you think we got ourselves into this crazy mess in the first place. Besides, we got to make them look like they're seniors."

"I don't know, Joe."

"You can have the first blind 'cause of your bad leg. I'll take the second one. We kill them, change clothes, drag the bodies into the woods, and stay in the blind until six."

"Maybe we could cut through the wire."

"Canada, Mason. They don't hunt seniors in Canada."

"Maybe there's a way to get over the fence."

Joe grabbed Mason's hands. "I won't wait for you, Mason. You can stay here and have your head blown all over the meadow if you want, but I'm going."

The backs of Joe's hands were covered with brown splotches. Mason looked at his own. "You think they still have a few horses in Canada, Joe?"

"Horses? Come on, Mason! You with me or not?"

There was fog in the meadow the next morning, which raised Mason's spirits immensely. He wouldn't have to move so fast. Each hunter was only allowed one bullet, and they wouldn't waste it in the fog. They would wait for the fog to lift, and, by then, he would be deep in the woods.

The fog was heavier in the trees, and Mason almost missed the blind. The sound of a lighter and the smell of a cigarette gave it away. Mason came up behind the blind. The hunter was dressed in a red plaid jacket. He had on a black wool cap and was sitting on a folding chair with a thick purple cushion, smoking a cigarette, his rifle across his lap.

As Mason watched, the hunter suddenly dropped the cigarette and grabbed the rifle. He thrust the barrel through the blind and looked into the telescopic sight.

The blast rocked the hunter back in his chair, and Mason heard him curse as he lit another cigarette. He had missed. Mason smiled and wondered who had been the beneficiary of the man's poor aim.

The hunter settled back in, and Mason saw his chance. He moved to his left and picked up a large rock. There was perhaps ten yards of open space, and, if he could get across that without being seen, he would have a chance. The hunter had used up his only bullet, but he was large and Mason was certain he couldn't kill the man with only his hands.

Mason had taken several steps toward the blind when the hunter reached into his pocket and took out a large box of shells. He opened the box and put a cartridge in the rifle.

Mason couldn't catch himself in time. "That's not

fair," he shouted. "One shell, God damn it. One fucking shell is all you're supposed to get."

The hunter spun around, falling off the cushion as he did.

Mason came forward with the rock in his hand. "You son of a bitch."

The hunter's hands were out in front of him, the palms pink and trembling. His voice was a hoarse whisper. "Don't . . ."

"One shell," Mason hissed. "One shell!"

The hunter began crawling deeper into the blind. He was sweating now, his face pulled white and contorted. "No," he said, pleading. "We all get a box." There was a bubbling sound to his speech as though he were being strangled. "Everybody gets a box."

Mason watched the hunter's face turn pale and translucent. The rock slipped from his hand. The pain in his leg was back. The hunter opened his mouth to say something more, but there was no sound. He stared at Mason for a moment, his mouth fluttering, as though he were on the verge of a great surprise. Then he grabbed his chest and arched backwards, his legs jerking out in front of him as he collapsed against the side of the blind. Mason stood there for a long time, rubbing the leg and looking down at the hunter.

It was Joe's voice that shook him out of his stupor. "Mason, Mason!" Joe was waving to him from the second blind. Mason nodded and waved back. His leg was aching now, the pain full of brilliant crystals. He moved the chair out of the way of the body and sat down.

From the blind, Mason could see down into the meadow. The fog was gone, and a fresh breeze was moving the grass. It was the same kind of meadow as was in the book. A meadow filled with brown and red and black horses, their shining bodies shimmering in the sun as they raced around and around. One bullet, damn it!

Across the meadow, Mason thought he saw something move in the woods. He strained to see, but the distance was too great. The hunter's rifle lay on the ground, and Mason picked it up and looked through the scope.

It was Mrs. Winchester. Mason could see her. She was trying to manoeuvre that walker of hers through the undergrowth. The metal leg of the walker appeared to be hooked on a vine, and she was trying to free it. Mason laid his face against the rifle and ran a hand along the stock. Mrs. Winchester was slightly out of focus, and he reached up and adjusted the sight. He could smell the soft gun oil and the stronger and more pungent smell of cordite. The metal trigger guard felt cool.

Mason smiled. Mrs Winchester had worked the leg loose and was shuffling off toward the ravine. Damn, he thought, she is a tough one. He put the crosshairs on her chest, let out half his breath, and squeezed the trigger. The bullet caught her in the spine, and the force of the shot carried her over the walker and down a slight embankment.

Mason watched her through the scope for a while. She lay face down in the trees, her bright pink dress looking for the world like a patch of wildflowers. Mason worked the bolt, ejecting the spent cartridge and driving in a fresh one. Ben Ingersoll was hiding in a hole under a large tree root, and all you could see was his head. It was a hard shot, Mason concluded, and he laid the rifle on the ledge to steady it. The top of Ben's head skipped off the root like a stone on a pond.

"Mason! Mason! What's the matter? What are you doing?"

Joe was halfway to the blind, running, waving his arms. "Canada, Mason, Canada! What the hell are you doing?"

Mason waved back and swung the muzzle of the rifle around and blew Joe's chest apart with a single shot.

Later that morning, Mason was able to locate Freddy Sharp, Amy Browning, and George Savage, and, for the rest of the day, he sat on the thick cushion, his bad leg stretched out in the green grass, working the bolt on the rifle until all the shells were gone, and the meadow ran with colour, as though the Ruby Hearts had come early.

Not Enough Horses

When Clinton Merasty showed up at Sarah Heavyman's place with the box, Sarah's father, Houston, was not particularly impressed.

"Kittens?"

"Kittens," said Clinton. "I want to marry your daughter."

"That's the way we used to do it in the old days, all right," said Houston.

"Yeah," said Clinton, "I know."

"Times change, I suppose," said Houston. "In the old days, when a man wanted to marry a woman, he'd bring horses."

When Clinton rang the doorbell on Saturday, he was carrying four boxes of honey-garlic sausages in his arms.

"Happy Canada Day," Clinton told Houston.

"Holy," said Houston, when he saw the sausages. "These are my favourite."

"They're from Rowe Meats."

"They're the best," said Houston. "You still want to marry my daughter?"

"You bet."

The following week, Clinton drove up with a brown, Naugahyde recliner. Clinton and Houston set it on the sidewalk in front of the house.

"This looks just like the chair your father has in his den."

"That's the one," said Clinton. "Dad said I could have it, if I thought it would help."

"What's your father going to sit on?"

"He bought a leather recliner at the Brick's half-price sale."

Houston eased himself into the chair and leaned back so he could catch the sun on his face.

"It's got this lever," said Clinton. "When you pull it, a footrest pops out and holds your feet up."

"It's comfortable, for sure," said Houston. "But your father's right. There's nothing like leather."

A few days later, Clinton came by with a snow blower in the back of his truck.

"It's July," said Houston. "You know something I don't?"

"Hard to find a snow blower once winter sets in," said Clinton.

"Is it new or used?"

"Used," said Clinton, "but it's got an eight-horse-power engine, six forward gears, and a twenty-six-inch clearing path."

"Eight horses, eh?"

"That's right."

"She's a good cook," said Houston. "I guess you know that."

"I do," said Clinton.

"And she's got a university degree in biology." Houston rolled the snow blower back and forth to check the balance. "Those things don't come cheap."

"I had the blades sharpened and the spark plug replaced."

"You love her?"

"Absolutely," said Clinton.

"You know," said Houston, "you've been by four times now."

"Yes sir," said Clinton.

"And four's an important number to Native people."

"Like the four directions?" said Clinton.

"That's right," said Houston. "A lot of the songs we sing are sung four times through, and a lot of the dances are done four times. Sometimes when we pray for something, we say the prayer four times."

"So, can I marry Sarah?"

"You should probably ask her."

"I have."

"What'd she say?"

"She keeps saying no," said Clinton. "I thought maybe you could talk to her."

"Yeah," said Houston, "that's what I would have said, too."

Clinton and Sarah were married in September. Houston would have preferred a traditional wedding on the reserve, but Clinton's parents were Catholic and insisted that the ceremony be held at the church in town.

Afterwards, Houston took Clinton off to one side. "I'm curious," he said. "How'd you get my daughter to marry you?"

"It wasn't easy," said Clinton. "I can tell you that."

"She ask about horses?"

"Yes sir."

"What'd you tell her?"

"I told her that there weren't enough horses in the world, but that I'd keep trying."

"Welcome to the family," said Houston. "You're smarter than you look."

That evening Houston relaxed on the recliner in front of the television with a plate of sausages on his lap, while the kittens fought over a twist-tie. He wasn't sure about the Catholic ceremony. A little too long, perhaps. A little too pretentious. The priest a little too pleased with himself. But all in all, it had been a fine wedding. Enough to eat, enough to drink. Plenty of cameras.

It was too bad about the horses, though. As Houston watched Tiger Woods sink a forty-five-foot putt, he wondered what it must have been like for his grandfather to stand in front of his lodge and feel the land tremble, as young men, wild for his approval, galloped by, driving strings of ponies through the prairie grass.

A snow blower was a fine thing, to be sure, but where was the romance, where was the tradition? Still, Houston had to admit, it did have an eight-horse motor, six forward gears, and a twenty-six-inch clearing path. And maybe tomorrow, if the weather took a turn for the worse, he'd run it to the backyard and start it up. Just to hear the motor rumble. Just to feel the earth move under his feet.

Noah's Ark

After Papa and William and Mary died, Mum took me and Luke to live with Granny. She had a squat, white stucco house hedged in by white and pink hydrangea bushes that leaned on the windows and blocked the light. There was a pasture behind the house and a creek, and, beyond the creek, Mr. Noah and the zoo. At night, you could hear the screaming, far away and in the dark.

On weekends, before Granny and Mum got up, Luke and I would slip out of the house and climb the fence into Mr. Thompson's pasture. There were cows in the field, brown ones with curly hair, and they would watch us, their big, stupid eyes rolled up and white, their heavy bodies leaning, ready to scuttle sideways or lurch off with their tails in the air down into the scrub and willow along the creek. They kept an instinctual distance, these cows. Most of the time, I ignored them.

The creek was brown and thick with oily weeds, and the high bank fell away to the bottom. The only place to cross was at the tree cut down by the spring floods. It lay completely on its side, but it hadn't died. Its roots were still buried deep in the earth, and the trunk bristled and twisted with new branches and soft layers of green sticky leaves. The zoo was on the flat above the creek, and we would scramble up to the grove of cottonwoods that stood near the bear pen and hang on the cyclone fence and watch the animals get fed.

Mr. Noah's red beard crackled and smoked in the morning frost, and his bald head glistened with sweat as he strode up and down between the cages, a metal bucket swinging from each arm. Back and forth between the iron cages and the zookeeper's house he went, the buckets filled to the top with chunks of bleeding meat or vegetables or grain or the dark, black-brown, foaming sludge that slopped over the lips of the buckets and fell in trailing pools behind him.

In the morning, the zoo was a riot of noise. The bears swayed and growled. The macaques stuck to the wire and then exploded, ricocheting around and around their cages. The geese and the ducks stampeded to the corner of their pen, honking and quacking, their necks craned in anticipation. The gibbons whistled, and the wild pigs howled and banged their teeth together.

"You think he'd kill us if he caught us looking?" Luke wanted to know.

I was older. "No, silly. They don't kill people for looking."

"Papa said they killed people in the war for looking."

"Those were spies."

"So?"

"We're not spying. We're just looking."

"They could still put you in jail or something," said Luke.

"Are you scared?"

It was a mysterious place, the zoo. "You know," I told Luke, "if any of those animals escaped, they would kill you. Every one of them is a dangerous killer. Mr. Noah is lucky to be alive."

"They like Mr. Noah. He feeds them."

"The bears would eat him so fast."

"What about the ducks? What about the monkeys? Monkeys don't eat people."

"Some do," I said.

"You know what Papa said about liars, Caroline."

"I'm not lying."

"They go straight to hell and rot."

Luke liked the cows. "The cows are nice. They don't eat anyone. They just eat grass."

"Cows are dumb."

"I think they are beautiful. They look real soft. Jimmy says if you put salt on your hand, they'll lick it."

"The bears would eat those cows in a second."

Papa was a preacher. He preached for the Nazareens and then he preached for the Baptists. The year before the accident, he went to preach for the Methodists in Loomis. The church gave us an old, two-storey house in the trees near the river. It had been newly painted—sky blue with yellow trim—and the kitchen had shiny pink linoleum squares filled with green and white flowers.

Mum said the cupboards were solid wood. Mary crawled into the stone fireplace in the parlour and said you could see all the way to the sky. We took turns looking up that chimney. It was true. You could see the sky, all right, a small patch of blue surrounded by darkness. Luke said it was like looking down into a magical well, but, if you stayed there long enough and your eyes adjusted, you could begin to see the edges of the bricks and the long streaks of soft, black soot on the walls. William said it smelled like vampire bats to him and that they really liked old chimneys. I didn't believe him, but he scared Mary and Luke.

After we brought the boxes in, Papa gathered us together, and we stood in the kitchen and held hands. "Thank you, God," Papa said, "for bringing us through the storm to this safe place. Thank you for this new beginning and for sharing your goodness and mercy with us, Amen." Luke and Mary found a board and William found a can of paint in the cellar and made a sign, but he spelled it wrong because he was too proud to ask me.

"Mum screams at night, Caroline. Sometimes it wakes me up."

"That's the zoo, silly. Whenever it gets dark, all the animals howl at the moon."

"The ducks don't howl."

"The real animals do."

"Cows don't howl, either."

"Cows are dumb."

"And she cries, too. Sometimes I can hear her crying."

"Animals love to howl at the moon, Luke. It sounds like screaming, but they're really having a good time."

Mum didn't cry when Papa died. Neither did I. Luke was too little to understand anything, so he didn't cry either. Mr. Bennett called to tell Mum what had happened, and she just sat down. It wasn't like in the movies at all. She told us to sit down, too, and then she said that there had been an accident and that Papa and William and Mary were with God. That was all that happened. There was the funeral, and we went to live with Granny.

It would be only temporary, Mum said when we got off the bus. We wouldn't be staying long. We had to walk to Granny's. Luke got to carry the green suitcase because he was smaller than me. "What if Granny doesn't want us?" Luke wanted to know. "Does she have a television?"

Mum carried the leather case, and we stopped at the end of each block to let Luke catch his breath. Everything was going to be good this time. Each time we stopped we sat on our suitcases, that's what Mum would say. We walked miles that day, dragging our bags along Ross Street until we got to Granny's house and stood on the porch in the shade and rang the bell and waited for her to let us in.

Granny smoked. You could smell it everywhere. And Mum said there was something wrong with her eyes but that we shouldn't ask her about it. Granny liked to sit in the kitchen and smoke.

"Those cigarettes sure do stink, Granny," Luke told her.

"You'll get used to it."

In the late afternoon especially, Granny would sit in a straight-backed chair in the kitchen, in the dark, and smoke.

"You're the man of the house, now," Granny told Luke. The blue smoke would curl off her cigarette and flow over her face and hair.

"I'm older than Luke."

"It's just a figure of speech, Caroline." Every so often, she would blow smoke out her nose, like frosty steam on a cold morning. "Luke's a boy, and you're a girl."

Mum got a job at the auction yards, at first. Then she worked for the Railroad Café across from the fire station.

"Why does Granny sit in the dark and smoke, Caroline?"

"Adults like to smoke."

"It smells awful."

"It's what adults do."

William hung the board on the fence. You didn't spell it right, I told him. He didn't care, he said. Everyone would know what he meant and sometimes there were different ways to spell the same word. Papa said he was going to borrow a camera and take a picture of all of us standing by the fence. But he never did.

That winter, the river flooded and put the fence under-water. We watched the sign slowly disappear, and, when the water receded, it was gone. As soon as the ground dried to a soft mud, we waded out to the fence. William had to carry Mary on his shoulders. Luke found the sign face down in the mud, and we cleaned if off as best we could and William nailed it back up. Mary thought we should say grace, so we did, and, after, as we trudged back to the house, William held the hammer above his head and sang "Onward, Christian Soldiers," and we all joined in.

"I don't believe you about the animals, Caroline."

"Okay. On Saturday, we can ask Mr. Noah."

"I don't like Mr. Noah."

"You're afraid of everything."

"I am not. I'm the man of the house."

"Boy, are you dopey. It's just an expression. That's all it is. It doesn't mean anything."

The new calves were in the field. We stood at the fence and watched them perched on their long, thin legs, leaning against their mothers. They had the same crazy eyes as the cows, and their mouths were full of white slobber. Luke sat on the fence and counted them.

"There are fourteen babies, Caroline. You see that brown one over there? Her name is Lucy."

"It looks like a bull."

"That one is Mabel. And that one is Mary."

"Come on," I said, "let's go see the bears."

"See how the mothers watch over them. I'll bet if we

tried to get close, the mothers would run us over and trample us to death."

"Come on. We're going to miss the feeding."

"Mum was screaming again last night."

"It's the animals you hear."

We had never even so much as said hello to Mr. Noah before. Some of the kids at school said he was real mean and had bad breath. He looked fierce all right, like the animals. Luke stood back a ways and watched the calves in the field, while I knocked on the door.

When Mr. Noah opened the door, he had a white apron tied around his middle and a butcher knife in his hand. He was even scarier up close, and you could smell the sweat. His beard shot out in all directions, and the hair around his mouth was lighter, as though he had sucked all the colour out of it. He was smiling, standing there with that knife. But it was his eyes you saw first. Clear, blue eyes, so bright and blue you could imagine that there were tiny fires burning behind them. He looked at me and then at Luke and then at me again, smiling all the while. Some of his teeth were missing.

"Well, children," he said. "Come in. I think you're just in time for some cookies. You children like cookies?"

Luke was behind me. "We like cookies," he said. And before I could stop him, he just walked into Mr. Noah's house. The house was light, and there were plants everywhere. The room smelled of apples and oranges and fresh-cut vegetables. "Come in, come in. What kind of cookies do you children like?" Mr. Noah sat us down at the kitchen table and brought us each four chocolate cookies and a glass of milk.

"I see you, you know," said Mr. Noah. "Hanging in the fence like little monkeys. You like to watch me feed the animals, do you?"

"I like the bears," I said.

"I'm glad you came around to say hello."

"The cookies were good, and the milk was cold. "My brother doesn't believe that animals howl at the moon."

Mr. Noah wiped his mouth with the red handkerchief. "Oh, they howl all right. They howl about everything. Just like people. They howl when they're hungry or when they're hurt or when they're scared. They even howl when they're in love. You children ever hear a bear in heat?

I shook my head.

"You children are old enough to know about this, ain't you? Your father ever tell you about these things?"

"Our papa was a preacher," said Luke.

"A preacher, huh? Well, then, you children must know the story of Noah's Ark."

"Sure. Our Papa was a Methodist."

"How the animals came on the Ark two by two?"

"Sure. Everybody knows that."

"How Noah looked after those animals like they were his own children? How he protected them from harm and fed them and cleaned up after them?"

"Just like you do, Mr. Noah?"

"That's right, children," said Mr. Noah. "Noah was the first zookeeper. The very first zookeeper in the world. Your father ever tell you that?"

"Our Papa's dead," said Luke. "William and Mary too. He was drunk."

"Luke!"

Mr. Noah shook his head. "Sorry to hear that," he said. "Animals die too, you know. Just like people. I lost a turkey last year. Old age. Lost a gibbon, too. Somebody shot her with an air pistol. I was real fond of her. Five of those young ones in the cage are hers. Every so often, at night, you can hear one of them crying."

"See," I said.

"Is it because they miss her?"

"Could be, child. Who knows why monkeys howl?"

"But animals howl at the moon, don't they?"

"Some do."

"Our Mum screams at night," said Luke.

"Always hard losing loved ones," said Mr. Noah, "always hard to go on without them."

"At night, I'll bet they howl loud enough so that we can hear them all the way to our house," I said.

"Most of them sleep at night," said Mr. Noah. "Just like us."

"We can hear them from our house."

Mr. Noah went to the cupboard and came back with a handful of raisins. He made two little piles on the table. "You kids know who makes the most noise around here? It's the cows out in that field. Sounds like a couple hundred tubas."

"Why do they do that?" asked Luke.

"It's when they bring in the bull," said Mr. Noah. "You best ask your mother about that."

We stopped at the field, so Luke could name some more of the calves. "Look, Caroline. They're having lunch. The one with the white patch is Cynthia."

"You shouldn't tell strangers about Papa, Luke."

"Mr. Noah is nice."

"Granny says we should forget the past."

"I miss Papa, Caroline. And William and Mary, too."

The sign stayed there until the night Papa came home singing, missed the driveway, and drove through the fence. He wasn't hurt. He was still singing when Mum and William went out and helped him back to the house. But the sign exploded into a thousand splinters. When you make a new one, I told William, spell it right, C-A-N-A-A-N, three A's. But he never did. He could see the bad times rising again.

"There are fourteen calves in the field, Mum," said Luke when we got home. "I've named ten of them. You want to see them?"

Mum was sitting in the kitchen, smoking, her eyes all red from the cigarettes. "It's okay, honey. Maybe tomorrow."

The calves grew quickly, and, instead of huddling by their mothers, they began running around the field like idiots, playing with each other. Luke would sit on the fence and watch them. One of them, Mary, according to Luke, came all the way over to the fence to let Luke pet her. "I didn't even have salt on my hand. Bet the bears wouldn't do that." On the weekends, when we crossed the field on our way to the zoo, the calves would bounce along behind us like rubber balls, all the way to the creek.

"I'm going to get a good job, soon," Mum said. "I've got my name in at the big companies in town. This is just temporary. We'll be back on our feet in no time."

"How come you cry at night, Mum?"

"That's a nightmare you're having, Luke."

"It's the animals at the zoo he hears," I said.

Mum got a job at the Woolworth's store, but she didn't stop smoking. When *Star Wars* came to town, we all went to see it. Granny, Mum, Luke, and me. Even Granny liked the movie. Mum bought a big bag of pop-corn, and Luke and me each got a medium soft drink.

We didn't hear the cows until we got home. Granny lit a cigarette and blew a silvery stream into the night sky. "They'll go on like that for days," she said. And she opened the porch and went in.

Luke and me stood in the yard and listened. It was the strangest sound, low and urgent, almost a wail, as though the cows were calling out to each other in the dark. Luke covered his ears.

"It's the bull," I said. "You're too young to under-stand."

The cows kept up the racket for the next couple of

nights. Granny said she could hear them all day long, that they never stopped. But, by Saturday, when we got up to go to the zoo, the cows were quiet.

The sun was low in the trees, when we got to the field. The grass was bright and wet, and the cows were moving through it, their heads dug in to the ground. They didn't even look up when we climbed the fence. Luke was the first to notice.

"Where are the calves?"

The calves were gone. The field wasn't very large. You could see along the fence line and all the way down to the creek. Luke walked out among the cows. "What happened to the calves, Caroline?"

"Maybe they had to move them. You know, when they brought in the bull."

"Why would they do that?"

"I don't know. Maybe they just did."

"Maybe someone stole them."

"Come on. We'll miss Mr. Noah feeding the bears. You can ask him about the calves."

But Luke didn't want to leave the field. He ran down and looked in the brush as if the calves were hiding in holes by the water. By the time we got to the zoo, Mr. Noah was already feeding the foxes. He saw us as we watched through the fence.

"Good morning to you!" he bellowed. "You children come to watch old Noah feed his family? They're hungry, today. Can you hear them roar?"

Mr. Noah put the buckets down. He wiped his hands

on his pants and came over to the fence. "When I'm done with the feeding, I might be able to find a few more of them cookies"

Luke looked back toward the field. "What happened to the calves, Mr. Noah?"

"The calves?"

"The calves in the field," Luke backed away from the fence. "What happened to the calves in the field?"

"Don't know for sure. Took them to the feed lot, I suspect," said Mr. Noah. "Thompson generally does that as soon as the calves are big enough."

"When do they bring them back?"

"Don't bring them back, son. They fatten them up and then it's off to the slaughterhouse."

"They don't kill them?"

Mr. Noah shook his head. "Where do you think such things as steaks and hamburgers come from?"

For the rest of the morning, Luke wouldn't come out of the field. He stood near the fence and watched the cows. I knew he was upset, and so was I, I guess, but I was hungry, too. Mum was in the kitchen when I got home.

"Hi, honey," she said. "Where's Luke?"

"He's watching the cows."

"Well, I've got something wonderful to tell the both of you."

"They took the calves in Mr. Thompson's field to the slaughterhouse, Mum. All of them."

Mum took a cigarette from her purse. "I got a job

today with the telephone company, honey. A real one. I have to take a week's training in the city. Granny's going to look after you and Luke while I'm gone. Maybe we can all go to a movie when I get back."

Luke came home later. We didn't talk about the cows. Mum told us all about her new job and how we might be able to get a television set for Christmas.

"We won't be able to get our house right away," she said. "That'll come later."

I had trouble getting to sleep that night. The air was humid with the promise of a hard rain, and, even with the window open, I was sticky and uncomfortable. I listened for the cows, but the field was silent. Later, I heard one of the gibbons cry out in its cage.

Where the Borg Are

By the time Milton Friendlybear finished reading Olive
Patricia Dickason's *Canada's First Nations* for a tenth-
grade history assignment, he knew, without a doubt,
where the Borg had gone after they had been defeated by
Jean-Luc Picard and the forces of the Federation. And he
included his discovery in an essay on great historical
moments in Canadian history.

Milton's teacher, Virginia Merry, was not as
impressed with Milton's idea as he had hoped. "Milton," she said, in that tone of voice that many lapsed
Ontario Catholics reserved for correcting faulty logic,
bad grammar, and inappropriate behaviour, "I'm not
sure that the Indian Act of 1875 is generally considered
an important moment in Canadian history."

"Why not?"

"But I am positive that there is no significant correla-
tion between the Indian Act and *Star Trek*." She said
this with the natural assurance that the well-educated
are able to manage, even though she had never read the

Indian Act and only knew about *Star Trek* because her husband watched it every night while they ate dinner.

"But it's all here," said Milton. "Pages two hundred and eighty-three to two hundred and eighty-nine."

"Your handwriting could use some attention," said Ms. Merry, and she wrote a note on Milton's paper in thin, delicate letters that reminded him of the doilies on the back of his grandfather's easy chair.

When Milton got home from school, he showed his paper to his mother, who sat at the table and looked at the grade for a long while. "Sixty percent's not too good, eh?"

"Ms. Merry said I have a vivid imagination."

"What's this about neatness?"

"That's because she's a Borg."

His mother read the paper, and, when she was done, she nodded thoughtfully. "Maybe you should go and talk to your grandfather."

Milton liked his grandfather a great deal and would have liked him just as much if he did not have a thirty-six-inch television set that was hooked up to the biggest satellite dish on the reserve.

"Hiya," said his grandfather. "You're just in time."

"*Star Trek*?"

"You bet."

"Are the Borg in this episode?"

"Who knows," said his grandfather. "It's always a surprise."

The episode did not have anything to do with the

Borg. It was about a hypnotic space game that would have turned the *Enterprise*'s crew into automatons had it not been for the quick thinking of Data and Wesley.

"I wrote a paper on the Indian Act," Milton told his grandfather as they waited for *The Simpsons* to come on. "For my history class."

"Oh, ho," said his grandfather. "I've heard about that one, all right."

"My teacher didn't think that it was a great historical moment."

"That's probably because she's not Indian."

"But I read this really neat book, and guess what?" Milton waited in case his grandfather wanted to guess. "I think I know where the Borg went after they were defeated by Jean-Luc Picard and the forces of the Federation."

"Boy," said his grandfather, "that's probably the question of the century."

Milton took his *Canada's First Nations* out of his backpack and put it on the coffee table next to his grandfather's recliner. "Everybody's been looking for them somewhere in the future, right?"

"That's right."

"But if this book is correct, I think the Borg went back in time."

"Ah," said Milton's grandfather.

"Into the past."

"Ah."

"Europeans," said Milton, and he turned to page two

hundred and eighty-four in the history book and pointed to the eighth word of the first line. "That's where the Borg went."

Milton's grandfather looked at the word just above Milton's finger. "Holy!" he said, and he sat up straight and hit the mute button.

"That's right," said Milton. "'Assimilation.' According to this book, the Indian Act is . . ." And Milton paused so he could find the right tone of voice. "An assimilation document."

Milton's grandfather picked up the book and turned it over.

"It was written by this woman," said Milton. "A university professor."

"Those women," said Milton's grandfather, "they know everything. Is she Indian?"

"She's Metis."

"Close enough," said Milton's grandfather. "Does that Indian Act say anything about resistance being futile? That would sure clinch it."

"So, you think I'm right about the Borg having come to Earth and taken over."

"It makes a lot of sense," said Milton's grandfather, "but I suppose we better get a copy of this Indian Act and read the whole thing before we jump to conclusions."

When Milton got home, his mother was waiting for him. "So," she said, "what did your grandfather think of your idea?"

"He liked it."

"You know, stuff like that might hurt people's feelings."

"It would explain why dad took off."

"It would, would it?"

"Sure," said Milton. "He was assimilated."

The next day, after school, Milton went to the library and looked up the Indian Act. There were all sorts of listings for Indians, but the act itself was not there. Milton looked under "Borg," too, but it wasn't there either.

"I'm looking for the Indian Act," Milton told the woman at the desk. "Do you know where I can find it?"

"Is it a . . . play?" asked the woman.

"I don't think so," said Milton, though he didn't know exactly what it was. "It's got to do with history."

The woman went to work on her computer and in a matter of minutes found the act. Milton was impressed.

"It's not hard," the woman explained. "This computer is connected to all the rest of the libraries in the province and to the National Library in Ottawa."

Milton began to feel a little queasy. "Sort of like . . . a collective?"

"Exactly," said the woman, who did not particularly look like a Borg. "Do you want me to request a copy of the act for you?"

"Oh, yes," said Milton.

"Is this for a school assignment?"

"Yes," said Milton.

"Research is fun, isn't it?" said the woman.

"It certainly is," said Milton.

* * *

The Indian Act didn't arrive right away. By the end of the second week, Milton figured that the Borg were on to him and that he might wind up disappearing the same way his father had. But when he got home from school the next day, his mother told him that the library had called. "They said to tell you that your *Indian Act* thing is in."

Milton raced down to the library. The woman was still sitting at the reference desk, and she smiled when she saw him. Beside her on the floor was a stack of rather large, very old-looking books.

"The Indian Act," she said, and she leaned over and gave the stack of books a pat.

"All that?" said Milton.

"No," said the woman. "These are the Revised Statutes of Canada for particular years. The original Indian Act is in the 1875–1876 volume. This one contains the revisions for 1886. This one is for 1906. There are a couple for the 1950s and one for 1970.

"Wow!"

"The Indian Act was revised a great many times."

"So it probably represents a great moment in Canadian history."

"I don't think so," said the woman. "Most great moments in Canadian history have holidays."

Milton looked at the stack for a few moments. "Okay," he said, and he began to stuff the books into his backpack.

"Oh, you can't take them out of the library," said the

woman. "These are government documents. They don't circulate."

Of course, thought Milton. The Borg wouldn't want their secret to get out.

"But you can xerox the parts that you need."

"How much is xeroxing?

"Ten cents a sheet."

Those Borg, thought Milton, as he hauled the books to one of the long tables by the window. They don't leave much to chance.

Milton spent the rest of the afternoon reading in each volume and taking notes. It was a long laborious process, but he was determined not to let the Borg and their ten-cents-a-sheet rule deter him. That evening, he showed his grandfather what he had found.

"What do you think?"

Milton's grandfather got up and stretched his legs. "I don't know," he said. "It sure sounds like the Borg."

"All the stuff about assimilation must be Borg," said Milton. "Look at this. 'Every Indian who is admitted to the degree of doctor of medicine, or to any other degree, by any university of learning, or who is admitted, in any province of Canada, to practise law, either as an advocate, a barrister, solicitor or attorney, or a notary public, or who enters holy orders, or who is licensed by any denomination of Christians as a minister of gospel, may, upon petition to the Superintendent, *ipso facto* become and be *enfranchised*.'"

"Whoa," said Milton's grandfather. "That could certainly limit the choices Native people might want to make."

"It sure could," said Milton. "I don't think I want to be . . . 'enfranchised.'"

"It sounds better than 'assimilated,'" said his grandfather, looking at Milton's notes. "But it's probably the same thing."

"So," said Milton. "What are we going to do?"

"It may be more complicated than we imagine." Milton's grandfather closed his eyes for a moment and then opened them. "Look at this section, 'The Governor in Council may authorize the Minister, in accordance with this Act, to enter into agreements on behalf of her Majesty for the education, in accordance with this Act, of Indian children.' Now that sounds more like the Vulcans than the Borg."

"You think so?"

"Sure," said his grandfather, "the Vulcans were always the intellectual ones."

Milton stood up and walked around in a circle. "You mean it was the Vulcans who came back in time?"

"It gets worse." Milton's grandfather sighed. "Look at this."

Milton leaned over his grandfather's shoulder. "Management of Indian Moneys?"

"And these." Milton's grandfather ran his finger down the notes that Milton had taken. "'Descent of Property,' 'Sale of Property,' 'Rent,' 'Sale of Timber Lands.' Who does that sound like to you?"

"Oh, no." Milton paled. "Ferengis?"

"Yep," said Milton's grandfather. "Sounds like we might be dealing with the Ferengis."

"And the Ferengi *Rules of Acquisition*?"

"Let's check it out." Milton's grandfather went to the bookcase and came back with a small notebook. "I've been keeping track of the Ferengi *Rules of Acquisition* in case there was something worth knowing."

"How many are there?

"At last count, there were two hundred and eighty-five."

For the next little while, Milton and his grandfather went through the Ferengi *Rules of Acquisition,* looking at each one carefully.

"Maybe you're right," said Milton. "Look at this. Rule Twenty-six. 'The vast majority of the rich in this galaxy did not inherit their wealth; they stole it.'"

"And Rule Twenty-seven," said Milton's grandfather. "'The most beautiful thing about a tree is what you do with it after you cut it down.'

"And Rule Forty-two. 'Only negotiate when you are certain to profit.'" Milton's grandfather shook his head. "Boy, I sure wish I had known about this before we signed those treaties."

Milton felt a shiver go up his spine. "Look at Rule Sixty-one."

Milton's grandfather ran a finger down the page. "'Never buy what can be stolen.'"

"You're right," said Milton. "The Borg didn't come back in time. And neither did the Vulcans. It was the Ferengis."

The next day Milton stayed after class and apologized to Ms. Merry. "I was wrong about the Europeans being Borg," he told her.

"It's all right," said Ms. Merry. "I'm sure it was an easy mistake to make."

"They're really Ferengis."

When Milton finished writing "Racism hurts everyone" on the blackboard fifty times, he went back to his grandfather's house to talk with him.

"I've been thinking," said Milton, "and something doesn't make sense."

"That's the trouble with life," said his grandfather. "Television is a lot simpler."

"It sure is," said Milton.

"So," said his grandfather, hitting the mute so he could still see what Captain Cisco and Dax and Quark were doing on *Deep Space Nine,* "what doesn't make sense?"

Milton put the Indian Act and the Ferengi *Rules of Acquisition* on the coffee table side by side. "We know that the Borg and the Vulcans and the Ferengis have little in common."

"That's true," said Milton's grandfather.

"I mean, the Borg want to assimilate everyone. The Vulcans want everything to be logical. And the Ferengis are only concerned with profit."

"I see your point," said his grandfather. "Europeans seem to have many of the bad habits of all three."

"They could be Klingons, too, because the Klingons are warriors and because Klingons love to fight simply for the sake of fighting."

"Don't forget those tricky Romulans," said Milton's grandfather. "Now that I think about it, those treaties have Romulan written all over them. What else does that Indian Act say?"

"Not much," said Milton, and he made a face. "It has a bunch of stuff about who's an Indian and who's in charge of Indian affairs and how you can get an Indian declared mentally incompetent."

"Boy," said Milton's grandfather, "if you were a Romulan, that would be a handy thing to know."

"So, what should we do?"

"Maybe you better talk to your teacher," said his grandfather. "And see if she can help us."

Milton wasn't sure he wanted to talk to Ms. Merry again, but he was very sure he didn't want to get her upset and have to spend the afternoon writing on the blackboard.

"Hello, Milton," Ms. Merry said with a cheery chirp, when Milton stopped by after school the next day.

"I have this problem," said Milton, glancing at the blackboard. "I was hoping you could help me with it."

Ms. Merry listened patiently as Milton explained what he had learned about assimilation and the Indian Act and how the Borg, or the Vulcans, or the Ferengis, or the Klingons, or quite possibly the Romulans, figured in the history of North America. Along with his theories on space travel, wormholes, and time warps.

"Christopher Columbus was not a Ferengi," said Ms. Merry. "He was an Italian."

"But you told us that he kidnapped Indians from the islands of the Caribbean and sold them in the slave markets in Seville."

"Yes, he did, but that doesn't make him a Ferengi."

"Who else but a Ferengi would try to sell people?"

"Milton," said Ms. Merry, "do you remember what I told you about racism?"

"Racism hurts everyone."

"That's right."

"I told my mother, and she mostly agreed with you."

"Mostly?"

"She said it hurts some people more than others."

That weekend, Milton's mother had to go to Edmonton for a conference. "You can come with me, or you can stay with your grandfather."

"Are you going to be near the West Edmonton Mall?"

"No."

Milton's grandfather was in the backyard setting up his tipi when Milton arrived with his backpack and his sleeping bag.

"Nothing like sleeping out under the stars," said his grandfather.

"Like the old days, right?"

"Right."

"Before television, right?

"You bet," said his grandfather. "Here, give me a hand with this."

"What is it?"

"An antenna. If you hook it to one of the lodge poles, it really improves the reception."

"We moving the big television outside?"

"No," said his grandfather, "it's too heavy."

Watching *Star Trek* on the seventeen-inch portable wasn't quite the same as seeing it on the big screen. But it was cozy inside the tipi, and during the commercials, if you looked up, you could see the stars.

"Look what I found," said his grandfather, and he handed Milton a magazine. "I went to the doctor's office the other day and there it was."

"Maclean's."

The banner headline on the cover said, "Abuse of Trust," and one of the stories was about the George Gordon Residential School in Saskatchewan.

"Residential schools," said his grandfather. "That's one of the places where Europeans tried to assimilate Indians."

"Are we back to the Borg, again?"

Milton's grandfather sighed and opened the magazine to page eighteen. "Look at this. It says here that in 1879 the John A. Macdonald government decided to set up boarding schools in order to remove Native children from their homes to begin assimilating them into white culture."

"And in 1894," said Milton, reading ahead, "Ottawa

passed an amendment to the . . ." Milton stopped for a moment to catch his breath.

"That's right," said his grandfather, "an amendment to the Indian Act making attendance for Native children mandatory at these schools."

"Wow!" said Milton. "So it was Borg, after all."

Milton's grandfather turned off the television and pulled the flap to one side. "Come on," he said. "I want to show you something."

It was a moonless night, and the sky was aquiver with stars. Milton's grandfather walked to the edge of the cliff overlooking the river and sat down on the prairie grass. "I think I know what happened," he said. "I think the Europeans and Jean-Luc Picard and the Federation are . . . one and the same."

"That's silly," said Milton, who did not really think of his grandfather as silly. "Europeans can't be part of the Federation."

"The Prime Directive, right?"

"That's right," said Milton. "The Federation's Prime Directive was never to interfere in the affairs of another race."

Milton's grandfather picked up a stick and drew a circle in the dirt. "You ever watch Sherlock Holmes on A&E?"

"It's a little slow," said Milton. "Mum likes it."

"Sherlock Holmes says that the way to solve a crime is to eliminate all the possibilities and then, whatever remains, however improbable, has to be the answer." Milton's grandfather paused and gestured toward the sky. "There's one."

Milton looked up in time to see a shooting star streak through the night.

"That's probably how it happened," said his grandfather. "That's probably exactly how it happened."

Milton was getting a little cold, and he was a little sleepy, and he had lost track of what his grandfather was trying to tell him. "We have anything to eat?"

"I got some apples."

"Any popcorn?"

Milton's grandfather shook his head. "Have you ever wondered why Europeans and the crew of the *Enterprise* look a lot alike?"

"Yeah, that is a little weird," said Milton.

"Europeans don't look like the Borg. They don't look like the Ferengis or the Klingons or the Vulcans or even the Romulans."

"Too bad Europeans aren't as nice and considerate as the crew of the *Enterprise*. I'll bet if Jean-Luc Picard had come to North America instead of Christopher Columbus, he would never have kidnapped Indians and sold them to other Europeans as slaves."

"Christopher Columbus did that?"

"Sure," said Milton. "You could make pretty good money selling slaves."

"Well, I guess that settles it," said Milton's grandfather. "It does."

"You're a smart boy," said his grandfather. "How would you explain a race of people who look exactly like Federation officers, but who want to assimilate everyone and make a profit at the same time."

If Milton had had any hair on the back of his neck he was sure it would be standing on end.

"Remember that episode when the Borg were racing toward Earth?"

"And everyone was chasing them?"

"Klingons, Ferengis, Vulcans, Romulans. And Jean-Luc Picard. Everyone travelling through space at incredible speeds."

"Warp ten at least."

"They go faster and faster. The Borg out in front. The Federation right on their heels." Milton's grandfather paused, so Milton could catch up.

"Like a shooting star."

"Exactly." Milton's grandfather nodded. "And then . . . something happened."

"Something?"

"An accident. And explosion. Maybe a wormhole collapsed."

"A wormhole! You think a wormhole collapsed and caught everyone in a high-energy gravity field?"

"Maybe it was a faulty temporal time warp," said Milton's grandfather. "Who knows."

"But everybody would have been . . . crushed."

Milton's grandfather shook his head. "Or they were phased into particle streams, and their atoms were mixed and merged. Borg, Klingon, Vulcan, Ferengi, Romulan, even Jean-Luc Picard and his crew."

"You mean they were . . . reconfigured?"

"And when the dust cleared, what do you get?"

Milton sat back and took a deep breath. "Europeans."

"Only thing that makes any sense," said his grandfather.

"This is worse than I thought," said Milton.

"I never did buy that story about Columbus sailing the ocean blue," said his grandfather.

"So what are we going to do?"

Milton's grandfather got up and brushed off his jeans. "Not sure there's anything we can do. I'll bet Europeans don't even remember it happening."

"You know what this means, don't you," said Milton glumly. "I'm probably going to have to write my paper over again."

For a Borg/Klingon/Vulcan/Romulan/Federation molecular composite, Ms. Merry was remarkably understanding. "No," she told Milton. "You don't need to do your paper over again."

"I know you can't help it," Milton told Ms. Merry. "It's just that I don't want to be assimilated."

"Then you should probably stop watching so much television," said Ms. Merry.

At the next community meeting, Milton's grandfather got up during the open microphone period and read Milton's paper out loud. It was a big hit, and, afterwards, several people came up and said it was nice to have a scholar on the reserve. Milton was flattered at first, but after he'd had a few cookies and some time to think, he felt a little depressed.

"What's wrong, grandson?" asked Milton's grandfather, as the two of them walked home under a spacious, starlit sky.

"I don't know," said Milton. "Doing that paper on the Indian Act and discovering what happened to the Borg was fun, but what good does it do to know that Europeans were created by a freak accident in deep space?"

"Probably not much," said his grandfather. "But look on the bright side. Now that we know the truth, having Europeans around won't seem nearly as bad as it once was."

"You think so?"

"Sure," said Milton's grandfather. "They invented television."

"That's true."

"And those ice cream bars covered with dark chocolate are pretty good, too."

"They certainly are."

Milton's grandfather stopped and looked into the sky just as another shooting star flashed through the night. "And don't forget the Borg."

"The Borg?"

"Sure," said Milton's grandfather. "Europeans are no great shakes, but think how bad things would have been for Native people if the Borg had gotten here in one piece." The old man paused for a moment and a frown began working its way across his face. "Unless, of course, we're wrong."

"Wrong about what?"

Milton's grandfather wrinkled his forehead. "Of course. That's what they want you to think."

"Who?"

"The Federation."

"Jean-Luc?"

Milton's grandfather sighed and sucked at his lips. "When has the Federation ever lost a fight? When have they ever lost anything?"

Milton thought about this for a moment. "Never."

"So, what if the deep-space accident never happened." Milton's grandfather was chuckling now. "What if the Federation attacked the Borg and defeated them long before the Borg got to Earth."

"You think the Federation attacked the Borg?"

"Why not. The Federation likes to fight as much as the Klingons."

"Yeah, but they never start the fights. The bad guys always start the fights."

"And they like logic, same as the Vulcans," said Milton's grandfather, "and they acquire things at almost the same rate as the Ferengis."

"Yeah," said Milton. "That's true. But what about the Prime Directive? The Klingons and the Vulcans and the Ferengis and the Romulans don't have a Prime Directive."

"Lot of good it does," said Milton's grandfather. "The Prime Directive says you're not supposed to interfere with another culture, but Jean-Luc Picard and Data and William Riker and Councillor Troy are always sticking their noses into other people's business."

"They can get a little pushy," Milton agreed. "Especially Riker."

"'To boldly go where no one has gone before,'" said Milton's grandfather. "Sounds like nosiness to me."

"That's just exploration talk."

"You know," said Milton's grandfather, "now that I think about it, the Prime Directive sounds an awful lot like the federal government."

"Our government?"

Milton's grandfather slapped his hands together. "You know what I think? I think that the Federation destroyed the Borg and then, when no one was looking, they ambushed the Klingons and the Ferengis, the Vulcans and the Romulans one by one, until there was no one left in the universe to oppose them."

"But why would they do that?"

"So they could have the universe all to themselves."

"But, Grandpa," said Milton, "the Federation are the good guys. Good guys wouldn't do something like that."

The smile on Milton's grandfather's face slowly faded, and the old man's shoulders sagged a little. "Holy," he said softly. "You're right. Boy, what was I thinking? I guess I got a little carried away."

"It's okay, Grandpa," Milton took his grandfather's hand. "It's an easy mistake to make if you don't know what you're looking for. All you have to remember is that, in most cases, the bad guys look like lizards or devils or scary people with dark skin and snaky hair."

"And the good guys look like Europeans?" said Milton's grandfather.

"Sure," said Milton. "Who else would they look like?"

The following Monday, Milton stopped by Ms. Merry's room to give her the good news and to ask her, in light of all the extra work he had done, if she would consider changing his grade.

"Collapsing wormholes and molecular realignment?"

"My grandfather thought it might be a tear in the space–time continuum, but he doesn't watch as much *Star Trek* as me."

When Milton's mother saw the new grade, she was pleased. "There's probably no one else on the reserve who knows as much about the Indian Act as you do. I never would have realized that it was such an important document."

Milton settled on the couch. Yes, he thought to himself as he ran through the channels until he got to Space, the Indian Act was an important document. Certainly important enough to have its own holiday. And who would have guessed, Milton mused as he watched Jean-Luc Picard save another primitive civilization from destruction, that it would turn out to be the key to understanding the universe.

States to Avoid

Avoid Utah.

Laura and I were living in Yuba City, and I told her I was willing to stay, that Yuba City was dull but in a nice, ordinary way, and staying wouldn't be a disaster like Vacaville or Modesto. But Laura said, "No, let's do what you want to do. You can't be afraid of change," she told me. "You've got to follow your dream." And, I could see her point, you know, I could see that things would be better this time.

So I said, "All right, let's go."

We packed our apartment, sold the stereo and the hide-a-bed, and said goodbye to our friends and the big valley oak in the backyard.

"You know what I'll miss most?" Laura asked me.

"The tree?"

"No."

"The apartment?"

"No."

It was Laura's plan to move. Well, not move out of Yuba City. That was both of us. But *how* to move to

Utah, that was Laura. She got a piece of cardboard and drew a diagram of the trip with coloured pens. I would drive the moving truck, and, since it was slower, I would have to leave earlier. Laura would follow in the car. The truck was a purple line. The car was a yellow line. The mileage from town to town was in green, and the rest stops—gas, lunch, coffee—were indicated in red. The motel where we were to stay in Elko the first night was a big blue dot.

"David and Sheila?"

"No."

"Helen and Tom?"

"No."

The night before we left, Helen and Tom and David and Sheila and Brad Glick, who worked with me at the office, came by to help us pack. Brad was in a jolly good mood.

"Damn, I envy you guys," he said. "What an adventure. Just pulling up stakes and starting over again. Wish I could do that."

Helen and Tom and David and Sheila weren't as happy and said that they would miss us, and they hoped things would work out.

"You guys will look back on this," Brad said, as we walked a table out to the truck, "and wonder why you didn't do it sooner."

The next morning, I left at six o'clock, and I have to say this for Laura's schedule: it was accurate. I was ten minutes early getting into Auburn, twenty minutes late getting out of Reno, and only five minutes late getting into Elko.

The Desert Flamingo was not as luxurious as the advertisement in the travel guide, but it had easy access to the highway and a wonderful pool that was teal blue and shaped like a pork chop with vinyl fish—sharks, catfish, swordfish, dolphins and whales—stuck to the side. One of the sharks was beginning to peel. That first evening of our move to Utah, while I waited for Laura, I floated in the pool until the fog began to drift in off the desert.

By eight o'clock, I was hungry. The man at the desk told me about a good restaurant, and I told him about the vinyl shark. He thanked me and said he'd tell Laura where I was when she arrived.

"The stereo?"
  "No."
  "The hide-a-bed?"
  "No."

I had the meatloaf. The waitress recommended it. Her name was Fay, and she was Paiute from the Reno area, and you could see she wasn't lying. All the white guys like the meatloaf, she told me. It was the chef's special, made with chopped red peppers, garbanzo beans, pine nuts, and raisins, not the kind of thing you find in a cookbook.

"The raisins keep it from going dry."

Fay had been married four times and was currently going through a divorce. She said most men were pigs, and she was always surprised to see a couple who had stayed married.

"Sometimes I think it's unnatural for two people to live together for more than five years," she said.

"Laura and I have been married eleven years."

"You got kids?"

"No."

"I got six. That's why I work here."

"For the kids?"

"For the money."

Fay was an interesting person. I enjoyed talking to her, and she was right about the raisins. When I got back to the motel, Laura still hadn't arrived.

I watched television for a while, and, at ten o'clock, I called the highway patrol. Then I called the hospitals in Reno. Then I called Brad to see if Laura had gotten off on schedule.

When Laura answered, I was greatly relieved, I can tell you that.

"Boy, am I glad to hear your voice," I told her.

"How did you find me here?"

"I called the highway patrol and the hospitals. What happened? The Dodge break down?"

"No."

"The battery, right? Damn I knew it wouldn't last much longer. Was it the battery?"

"I didn't leave."

"Okay, just so long as you're safe. I'm in Elko. I'll wait until you get here. What's wrong with the car?"

"Nothing is wrong with the car."

My room faced the highway. I could hear the big trucks rumble by in the fog. The ones going east were headed to Utah, just like me.

"So," I said, "when do you figure you'll get here?"

"I'm not coming."

I had never thought of fog in the desert. Yuba City had lots of fog, really dense stuff, but I guess I expected the desert would be clear. Just one of those little surprises in life. I could barely see across the parking lot.

"Utah isn't that bad, honey."

"It's not Utah."

"There's good skiing in the mountains, and Salt Lake City is supposed to be very progressive."

"It's not Utah."

"Hey, you'll never guess what the weather is like here in Elko. Fog. You believe that?"

We talked for a while, and I remember her sounding tired as though she had driven for hours. But, of course, she hadn't. Finally she sighed as if the air was slowly being pulled out of her.

"Here," she said. "Why don't you talk to Brad."

I talked to Brad, who said he was glad I had made it to Elko safely, and that driving in fog was a dangerous thing at best. I told him about the meatloaf and the raisins, and he said he'd have to try it. He told me a funny joke about truck drivers and rabbits, and said I should call back tomorrow when Laura wasn't so exhausted.

"Okay, I give up. What are you going to miss most?"
"Think about it for a minute. Just think about it."

When I returned to the restaurant, Fay was still behind the counter. I sat on a stool.
"Hi," I said.
"Coffee?"
"Sure."
"You want to see a menu?"
"I just ate. I had the meatloaf. Remember, we talked about marriage."
Fay smiled. "I must have been drunk. Leroy's party, right?"
"What?"
"Did Leroy put you up to this?"
"Who's Leroy?"
"Well," she said, pulling at the pen in her apron, "I'm not going to marry you. The meatloaf is good tonight."
"I had the meatloaf. Remember me. I'm the guy from Yuba City. My wife and I are moving to Utah."
She said, sure, she remembered, and I ordered some coffee and a piece of pie and a large order of french fries. We talked in between customers, and, after a while, we got to be friends.

"I get off at two. Why don't you come by my place. I got some pizza I can throw in the microwave. I want to hear more aboout this Brad guy."

Fay lived in a single-wide trailer. I had always thought of trailers as those little silver things that looked like metal sow bugs, but Fay's place was almost spacious. I mean, it was skinny, but it was also long. I told her I liked it, and she told me she was renting it from the guy who owned the restaurant.

"So this guy named Brad has been fooling around with your wife."

"No, that's not it. She's just trying to find herself."

"Seems to me, she has."

"I'm going to call her tomorrow. She's upset that we had to move. What do you think I should say?"

"Probably just as well you don't have any kids."

The pizza was chewy but good. Fay had some beer in the refrigerator, and it helped wash the pizza down.

"Not to be crude or anything, but he's probably banging her right now, you know."

"It's not like that at all."

"You white guys are as dumb as hell."

I liked Fay, you know. She spoke her mind. I always had to guess what Laura was thinking, and she kept things in her. Fay just said whatever came to mind. She told me about her latest husband, and how she had caught him in bed with one of the other waitresses.

"In this trailer?"

"Where else did you think he'd go?"

"What about the kids?"

"I just say that for the tips."

Around four in the morning, I had my heart attack. It started out as a burp, and then the pain came. Fay helped me out to her car.

"Hang on, honey," she said, which made me feel loved in a nice way. "You want me to give your wife a call? Women are suckers for heart attacks. I flew all the way to San Diego when my second husband had his first heart attack."

Fay drove me to the hospital, and they strapped me up to a couple of machines. Fay ran around yelling at people as though she owned the place.

"The man's dying, for christ's sake. How about some service?"

I would have guessed that, if you knew you were dying, you would spend your time thinking about the people you loved and how much you would miss them and how much they would miss you. But lying on that table with all those people running around me, all I could think about was the truck and whether I should go on to Utah or go back to Yuba City.

Fay was there the whole time. She got one of those large styrofoam cups of coffee, pulled up a chair near the bed, and told me about each of her four husbands. And, after a while, my chest didn't hurt so much.

As it turned out, it wasn't a heart attack. All the tests were normal, and the doctor said it was probably a bad case of heartburn or the symptoms of a possible hiatal hernia, and that, if it happened again, I should get it checked out.

"What did you have for dinner?"

"Meatloaf and pie."

"Anything fatty or greasy?"

"Some french fries."

"You drink coffee?"

"Couple of cups."

"Anything else?"

"Pepperoni pizza."

"You can still digest that stuff?"

"My wife just left me, too."

"You're kidding. Pepperoni?"

"So, it's not a heart attack?"

The doctor gave me a short lecture on the dangers of stress and how I should try to avoid it. She also gave me a list of foods I should avoid eating, especially late at night.

By the time we got out of the emergency room and Fay dropped me off at the motel, it was after eight.

"Don't lose sleep over what's-her-name," said Fay. "She's probably still in bed with a smile on her face."

"We'll get things worked out," I told her.

"You and all the king's horses and all the king's men."

The truck was still in the parking lot. The fog was gone, and the air was cold. I was starting to shake. "Thanks for taking me to the hospital and staying with me," I said. "I owe you one."

Fay smiled and blew me a kiss and shook her head. "Humpty Dumpty." And she rolled up the window and drove away.

All things considered, I think lying is a bad idea. People will argue with you about this, but my feeling is that if you lie and you are believed, then you have to continue the lie, which is difficult, and that if you are not believed, then you feel foolish. When I told Laura about my heart attack, she sounded concerned.

"It wasn't major," I told her. "Just a small one."

"My God," she said. "Shouldn't you be in the hospital?"

"I was there most of last night. They said I could go home, but that I shouldn't drive or go anywhere for a week or so."

"You only have the truck for six days."

"I know."

She was concerned. You could hear it in her voice. In my defence, I have to say that I thought it was a heart attack. Now that's the truth.

"What are you going to do?"

I told Laura that the heart attack had given me a new view of life, that there were important things and unimportant things. The truck was unimportant. Relationships were important.

"What's important is us," I said. "I can come home or we can go to Utah. As long as we love each other."

Laura didn't say anything, but I could hear her breathing into the phone.

"Don't cry," I said.

"I'm not crying."

"Do you think we can still get the apartment back?"

"Here," said Laura. "Maybe you should talk to Brad."

I slept most of the day. By the time I got up, I was hungry. The guy at the motel was cleaning the pool. He waved at me and asked if my wife had arrived yet. The restaurant was almost empty.

"You again," said Fay. "How's what's-her-name?"

"She's fine."

"What'd you do to make her so angry?"

"I didn't do anything."

"That will do it every time. You tell her about your heart attack?"

"It wasn't really a heart attack."

"Okay, so shoot me."

Fay recommended the french dip sandwich, and she said she'd substitute cottage cheese for the fries.

"So, what are you going to do?"

"I thought I'd go home."

"That's real smart."

"Well, I can't stay here."

"That's for sure. I've got enough troubles already."

That night, I went home with Fay, and we made love. "There are four things you should avoid in life," Fay told me afterwards.

"I've never done this before, but it was nice."

"I don't have to tell you the first one."

"Actually, it was great."

"And number two is pretty obvious."

"I really mean it."

"You can guess what three and four are."

"It sort of reminded me of when Laura and I were first married."

"So, don't get any funny ideas. Think of it as therapy."

"Thank you."

"Not for you. Christ. For me."

When I woke up in the morning, Fay was gone, but she left me a note that said she had the next two days off and that she was going to visit her daughter in Reno. Lock the door, the note said, and good luck.

I went back to the motel and phoned Laura, but there was no answer.

"So what are you going to miss most?"

"If you knew, you wouldn't have to ask."

The vinyl shark had come loose and was floating in the pool. The guy at the desk said he'd tell the maintenance people. "Your wife ever show up?"

"She was delayed."

"Happens a lot around here."

"How far is it to Utah?"

"Is that where you're heading?"

The waitress's name was Terri. She recommended the stew. It came with steamed vegetables and mashed potatoes and a dinner roll. I told her I was a friend of Fay's, and that my wife and I were moving to Utah. She said she had never been to Utah and had never been married, for that matter, but she had heard it was a nice state to be in.

Fire and Rain

I should tell you from the outset that I am a man who has been married. I should further say that I was happily married. Content. Relaxed. Fulfilled. My wife left me. No, no need to say you're sorry. It happened months ago, and if it wasn't for James Taylor, I wouldn't even mention it at all. Yes, of course, the singer. Yes, the guy who was married to Carly Simon but isn't now.

Suzanne had an affair. All right, she had several affairs. No, not with James Taylor. You're not listening. I don't know exactly how many affairs she had. They just happened.

"I love you, Suzanne."
"I know."
"Do you love me?"
"Sure."

* * *

Well, what was she supposed to say? Put yourself in her position. Can you really believe that she would say she didn't love me? Can you imagine how uncomfortable that would have been? Besides, Suzanne did love me. Not all the time, but then who does? It's so obvious. I don't know why you'd even ask. After you've lived with someone for fifteen years, love becomes less chaotic, more regular, ordered. Love takes on a rhythm. Take out the garbage. Cut the lawn. Pay the phone bill. Love your spouse. Yes, it does. No one likes to admit it. And there's nothing wrong with order. I know words such as "comfortable" and "secure" are out of fashion, and that's not what I mean anyway. I'm talking about love.

"I really love you, Suzanne."
"I love you, too."
"Really?"
"Sure."

Of course, there are problems with marriage. Whoever said there are no problems? For example, trying to do things together can be a trial. Always trying to do things together. As a family. It's silly, really. You do it because you love each other. Now, as a single man, I can go anywhere I wish. I can go to a ball game. I can go to the symphony. I can go to an art opening. I have not done any of these things yet, but I could do them whenever I please. Marriage is not as selfish.

"You want to go for a walk?"
    "Okay, whatever you like."
    "There's a good show on television."
    "Sure."

The other night, as a single man, I went to a movie. I forget the name of the movie because I did not go. I should have said I meant to go, but when I got to the movie, I discovered that the next show didn't start for an hour and a half. This did not happen when I was married, and I mention it simply as an example of the new freedom I am enjoying. When I discovered that I was either late or early for the show, I decided to go for a walk. I could have sat down in a café and ordered a cup of coffee. I could have gone to the magazine store on the corner. But I said, no, I'll do these things later. Right now I want to walk. So, I did.

"You know, I love you more now than I did when we were first married."
    "That's sweet."
    "It's true."
    "That's sweet."

* * *

So I went for my walk and as I was walking, I could see a crowd at the end of the block Why don't you see what that crowd is all about, I said to myself. I didn't have to ask anyone else about this matter. Well, you won't believe this; the crowd was waiting to get into the James Taylor concert. James Taylor. I love James Taylor. When I was first married, I bought a James Taylor record that was on sale. It was his *Greatest Hits*. God, what a wonderful record. Suzanne and I played it and played it. "Just yesterday morning, they let me know you were gone . . ." "In my mind I'm going to Carolina . . ." Yes, that's exactly what happened. I was standing there looking at the crowd and the flashing marquee, and I started singing James Taylor. Not out loud. Softly. To myself.

Of course, the concert was sold out. Can you really imagine a James Taylor concert that wasn't sold out?

So there I was, looking at the crowd, men and women, arm in arm, filing into the James Taylor concert, loving each other, happy, and I wanted to go to that concert. I didn't want to go to the show anymore. I wanted to go to *that* concert. And as I thought these thoughts, as they welled up in my brain, at the very instant they appeared, a man magically pushed his way through the crowd. And in his hand, between his thumb and first finger, was a single ticket for the concert. He wasn't holding up two tickets. He was holding up one ticket. A ticket for James Taylor. A ticket for a man who used to be married but now was not.

"How much?"

"Twenty dollars."

"Is it a good seat?"
"Sure."

It *was* a good seat. It was a wonderful seat. My God, it was in the second row in the orchestra pit. I was fifteen feet away from the stage, twenty feet from where James Taylor was going to stand. Pay attention. These things don't happen to you when you're married. You may think that I'm soured on marriage, but it's not true. I liked being married, and I may get married again. It was Suzanne who left. And don't think that I wasn't upset about the affairs. I was. But I forgave her those. She left in spite of my forgiveness. I told her I could forget the affairs, that life was too short to hold onto something so insignificant.

"Suzanne, I forgive you."
  "Are you sure?"
  "Sure."
  You see? I insisted on forgiving.
  "As long as you love me."
  "Of course I love you."
  "Are you sure?"
  "Of course."

*   *   *

One day I was married, and then I wasn't. One day I went to a movie and wound up at a James Taylor concert. You see what I mean? Life is like that.

The concert was fabulous. James Taylor stood twenty feet away from where I was sitting and sang. All those songs. Every one of them. What a voice! I was so close, I could see his fingernails as they struck each of the six strings on the guitar. And I could see his eyes open and close. We brought him back for four encores. I'm not exaggerating. My hands were bruised from clapping. The whole audience stood, and we stomped our feet and clapped our hands. I was there. I was part of it. JAMES . . . JAMES . . . JAMES. We were shouting and clapping and stomping. And he came back. God bless him! He came back and sang another song and another. My face was wet. It's true. I was crying.

I used to cry about Suzanne. It was love. I was so happy. She made me so happy. I would cry after she went to bed so I wouldn't bother her. Sing me another song, James. "Suzanne, the plans we made put an end to you . . ." When the concert was over, I just stood there in the aisle. The people made their way to the exits and I watched the crew tear down the stage. They moved the speakers and lifted the platform. They unplugged microphones and rolled up the cords. They worked so fast. Hardly any sound. And the stage began to vanish. It was sad.

And then in that boil of activity and bodies, wires, boxes, screens, drums, guitars, electronic keyboards, microphones, backdrops, chairs and stools, there he was. James Taylor. He was talking and laughing with the crew. What a guy! And I had my program and, right then and there, I decided to get his autograph. The perfect end to a perfect evening. Suzanne would have killed for James Taylor's autograph. If I get James Taylor's autograph, Suzanne will come back to me. You believe it? That's what I said to myself. And let me tell you, it wasn't the first time I had made a deal. Don't look at me like that. And, no, I don't think it's unnatural. People do that sort of thing all the time. Make promises. To God. To ourselves. To other people. You know it's not *going* to work. It's just something you say.

"If I get James Taylor's autograph, will you come back?
  "Yes, I will."
  "Are you sure?"
  "Sure."

I walked back down to the stage. I strolled along looking at the proscenium arch, at the murals on the walls, at the seats. He didn't see me, and I was waiting for him as he came across the stage. He came right at me. He saw me with my program and my pen. He knew me, and he was coming. No rush, James! Great show! Love your songs!

He jumped right off the stage and into the orchestra pit. James Taylor was standing two feet away from me, and I smiled. I was beaming.

* * *

"Mr. Taylor, could I have your autograph?"

"Sure."

And he walked over to where a small group of people were standing. They must have been friends. He kissed one of the women and had his picture taken with one of the men. And then he left. He left.

"Mr. Taylor, could I have your autograph?"

"Sure."

"Suzanne, do you love me?"

"Sure."

In all fairness, he probably just forgot. He was going to say hello to his friends and then come back and sign my program. So I waited. But he didn't come back. I knew he'd remember later and feel terrible.

I walked home. I could have taken a bus or a taxi, but I decided to walk, and I started thinking about Suzanne and how it had been. "Deep greens and blues . . ." Those were good days, but there were good days ahead, too. Maybe I would write James and tell him it was okay, that I knew he forgot and not to worry about it. I know, one day, we'll meet again, and he will look at me and smile and say, "God, I'm sorry. I forgot all about you. I can't believe I walked out and left you. Can you forgive me?"

I'll take him in my arms. I'll take him in my arms and hold him. That's the way it will be. Me and James. "Sure," I'll say. "Sure."

Rendezvous

On the morning of the first day, the skunks appeared in the garden as Evelyn Doogle was having morning tea under the tree.

"You should have seen it," she told her husband, when he got home that night. "A mother and four babies. Paraded right past me as if they owned the place."

Alistair Doogle wasn't at all sure about skunks parading through the backyard. "Fred and Lucille had skunks under their deck last year," Alistair told Evelyn, "and it took months to get rid of them."

The raccoons showed up that evening, pulled the plastic cap off the roof vent, and settled in the attic. Alistair could hear them scrambling around the rafters as he watched *Monday Night Football*.

At halftime, Alistair got a broom from the kitchen, and, during the commercials, he banged one end against the ceiling, and barked like a dog. Then he walked over to Durwin Milroy's house.

"I need to borrow your ladder," he told Durwin.

"Fred has it," said Durwin. "He's got raccoons in his attic."

"So do I," said Alistair.

"Now that's weird," said Durwin. "So do I. You want some coffee?"

Alistair and Durwin sat on Durwin's front porch in the dark and watched a coyote chase a cat down the block.

"It's been like this all week," said Durwin. "There are antelope on the golf course."

"Antelope?"

"Didn't you hear?" said Durwin. "They had to close the back nine."

"What the blazes are antelope doing in the city?"

"Don't know," said Durwin, "but the real problem is the wolf pack in the park."

The next day, deer began appearning on city streets along with badgers, a family of wild pigs, a herd of mountain goats, and several pairs of wood ducks, who took a liking to Judy Melville's swimming pool.

"They're lovely," said Judy. "All those bright colours, but I really can't have them doing their business you know where."

That afternoon, the mayor called a town hall meeting to discuss the problem, and when Alistair and Evelyn arrived he was introducing a dark-haired man in a pin-striped suit.

"This is Mr. Wagamese," said the mayor. "From the Department of Natural Resources."

"About time," said Durwin. "This nature thing is getting out of hand."

"An Indian," Alistair whispered to Evelyn. "Now we're getting somewhere."

The Indian set up a series of graphs and charts on a stand and turned on a slide projector. "We've always lived with animals," he said, "pigeons, seagulls, crows, rabbits, mice, rats, dogs, cats."

"Oh yeah," said Harry Austin, "well, I have a wolverine in my gazebo."

"Moose," yelled John Wright from the back of the room. "Two cows and a calf."

"For crying out loud," thundered Mabel Massey, who had recently retired from the stage in Toronto and could still fill a room with her voice, "this isn't a contest."

"Quite so," said the Indian, "and it's only going to get worse."

"Worse?" said Harry Austin. "What could be worse than having a wolverine in your gazebo?"

"Moose!" yelled John Wright. "Two cows and a calf."

Which started another round of comparisons.

"We've been warning you about this for years," said the Indian, and he brought up a new slide.

Alistair had no idea what he was looking at and from the silence in the hall, neither did anyone else.

"This is the boreal forest surrounding the Churchill River," said the Indian. "Twenty years ago it was a pristine wilderness."

"What are all those lines running through it?" asked Alistair.

"Roads," said the Indian. "Those lines are roads."

"And those dark squares," said Alistair. "What are they?"

"Resorts," said the Indian.

"Skiing?" said Alistair.

"Yes," said the Indian.

"Golf?"

"Yes."

"So," said Alistair, "what's the problem?"

Alistair was not in a good mood, as he and Evelyn drove home. "I still don't see what the problem is," he said. "Roads and resorts don't take up much space."

"Do you think he was right?" said Evelyn.

"Of course not," said Alistair. "It's just an aboriginal scare tactic to get us to recycle and use less electricity."

"What about Algonquin Park?" said Evelyn "Look what happened to Algonquin Park."

Up the block, Alistair could see several owls perched on the street signs, watching a family of rabbits work their way through the flower beds in front of the Peaceable Kingdom Funeral Home.

"Old news," said Alistair. "No sense dwelling on the past."

One of the owls slid off the street sign, pounced on a rabbit, and began ripping it to pieces.

"Remember that show we saw about how we were destroying the ocean?" said Alistair. "Well, the ocean is still there, isn't it?"

"I don't know," said Evelyn. "We haven't been to the ocean in years."

The next morning, Alistair was awakened by a loud hammering against the side of the house. Evelyn was standing in the driveway with a field guide in her hand.

"What the hell is all the noise?" said Alistair.

"Up there," said Evelyn. "Isn't it beautiful?"

On the side of the house was a huge black and white bird with a flash of red on its head. As Alistair watched, the bird used its beak to hammer a hole in the siding.

"It's a pileated woodpecker," said Evelyn, holding up the guide so Alistair could see the picture. "You normally don't see them in cities."

"What the blazes is it doing?"

"Looking for bugs," said Evelyn.

"We don't have bugs in our siding."

At the town hall meeting, the chief of police gave a talk on public safety and suggested that going for walks in the evening was not a good idea.

"Apparently," he told everyone, "a number of large predators are nocturnal. If you want to go for a walk after dark, it would be best to do it in your car."

"What kind of a walk is that?" said Evelyn.

"Then go for walks in large groups," said the chief of police. "Mountain lions have trouble focusing on individuals moving in a large group."

"Mountain lions?" said Alistair.

"In the parking lot at the mall," said the chief of

police. "I just made it back to my car in the nick of time."

"What was a mountain lion doing in the parking lot at the mall?"

"Stalking the buffalo in front of the Old Navy store," said the chief of police.

"That Indian still around?" said Alistair. "I think we should talk to him again before this thing really gets out of hand."

Everyone sat right where they were and discussed the upcoming home and garden tour while they waited for the police chief to find the Indian. This time he didn't have his graphs or his charts or his slide projector with him.

"He doesn't look happy," said Evelyn.

"He's just being stoic," said Alistair. "I've seen it before."

"The animals are becoming a public nuisance and health hazard," said the mayor. "We need to know how to get them to go to back to the forest."

"That's what I've been trying to tell you," said the Indian. "The forests are gone."

"That's nonsense." said Harry Austin. "We drive through forests every time we go to our cottage."

"No," said the Indian. "That's just a hundred-yard strip along each side of the road that the timber companies were required to leave."

"This is beginning to sound like environmental belly-aching," said Durwin Milroy. "What we need to know is how to get rid of the animals before someone gets hurt."

"That's right," said the mayor. "Forests or no forests, we can't have wolves annoying our citizens."

Later that evening, Alistair and Evelyn sat in the living room and listened to the wolves and the foxes and the moose and the hawks and crows and magpies and watched as a herd of elk, silhouetted against the setting sun, wandered past their picture window.

"It's a little noisy," said Evelyn, "but having wild animals in the city is rather exciting, don't you think?"

Alistair watched as the elk moved from one lawn to another, churning up the grass with their hooves and plowing through the flower beds. He had to admit that there was a kind of National Geographic feel to the moment, but he knew that it would pass, and, in the end, he was sure that this new arrangement would never work. Living with the occasional skunk or raccoon was one thing. Living with a herd of elk in your yard, majestic though they might be, was quite another.

The next morning, while he was watching an old rerun of *The Rockford Files*, Alistair realized that he couldn't hear the raccoons in the attic anymore. He turned down the volume and listened for a while. Then he went into the garden.

"Honey," he said to Evelyn. "I think the raccoons are gone."

"That's not all," said Evelyn. "Lucille says her wood ducks have disappeared."

"The coyotes probably ate them," said Alistair.

"Nope," said Evelyn. "They're gone, too. No skunks, either. And I heard on the radio that they've reopened the back nine at the country club."

Just after lunch Durwin Milroy and Harry Austin stopped by.

"How's the wolverine doing?" said Alistair.

"Vanished without a trace," said Harry.

"Crows are gone, too," said Durwin. "So are the hawks and the magpies. Haven't even seen a sparrow."

"Hey," said Alistair, "maybe the pigeons will be next." And everyone had a good laugh.

"I don't know," said Evelyn. "Now that I think of it, I haven't heard a bird all day."

"She's right," said Durwin. "It's real quiet."

"About time," said Alistair. "All that noise was keeping me awake."

"You think they're gone for good?" said Durwin.

"One can only hope," said Alistair.

Bright and early the next morning, Alistair and Evelyn headed up to the cottage, and, when the road began to wind its way through the forest, Evelyn had Alistair pull over.

"I'm just curious," she said.

"Worth a look, I guess," said Alistair. "But Indians do tend to exaggerate."

Alistair and Evelyn walked through the trees and

came out into an open field of stumps and slag piles for as far as the eye could see.

"I'll be darned," said Alistair. "The Indian was right."

"So, what are we going to do?" said Evelyn, as they walked back to the road.

"These things come and go in cycles," said Alistair. "I wouldn't worry about it."

That evening, Alistair and Evelyn sat on the deck overlooking the lake and waited for the loons to begin their haunting serenade. But that night and the next, the lake remained silent. Not even the mosquitoes came out of the cedar bush to annoy them as they sat in their chairs and watched the sun sink into the water.

And on the morning of the seventh day, they drove back to the city.

Domestic Furies

My mother always wanted to be the heroine in a play, a strong woman who rose above adversity or held her family together during desperate times or died beautifully of something that wasn't contagious or embarrassing.

She could have been an actress, she liked to tell me, and I believe that this is true, for she would move around the beauty shop as if she knew where to place each foot, when to turn, how to hold her head so that her hair caught the light that came in through the plate-glass window.

On Sunday mornings when the shop was closed, my mother would go out behind Santucci's grocery and pick any flowers that Mrs. Santucci hadn't been able to sell. Most of them were in pretty bad shape, but she would trim the stems, cut off the dead parts, and arrange them in the green vase and put them in the front window. Then she would warm up the Philco hi-fi my father had bought just before he left and load a stack of records on the spindle. They were musicals for the most part or operas, *The Desert Song, Carmen, The Student Prince, La Traviata, South Pacific,* and *Indian Love Call.* She knew all the songs by heart, and her voice blended in so well with the record that you could hardly tell them apart. She followed the music around the house until all the records had dropped onto the turntable. Then she would turn off the phonograph with a quick, hard gesture that reminded me of my grandmother wringing the heads off chickens.

My father hadn't gone very far. He kept a small apartment out by the auction yards, and most Friday afternoons after school, I would go to his place.

"How you doing?"

"Fine."

"How's your mother?"

"She's fine."

"She got any boyfriends?"

"Nope."

"You'd tell me if she did, right?"

"Sure."

Once every month on Saturday morning, he would take me to Eddie Bertacci's barbershop for a haircut. There were four chairs in the shop, though Bertacci worked alone and only used the one chair near the front window. He was a short, dark man with knotted red hair and a thin line of a moustache so black and dense it made his lip look as if it were hiding under a ledge. My father told me that Bertacci had put in the other three chairs for each of his sons, but that all of them had taken off. There were postcards stuck around the mirrors.

"Danny's in Italy now," he said, pointing to one of the cards. "Joey's working for Rockwell in Los Angeles. That one's from Mario. He came through last month."

Mr. Bertacci pointed to one of the palm trees and the ocean running up on the beach. "What d'ya think? Pretty nice, huh?"

"Is that Hawaii, Mr. Bertacci?"

"Who the hell knows."

The writing on the back of the cards was all the same, tiny, crunched letters that you couldn't read.

"Whatcha gonna do when you grow up?"

"Don't know."

"Hey, Leo, what's this boy of yours gonna do when he grows up?"

"Why don't you ask his mother."

"Well, ain't that the shits."

Mr. Bertacci said he had cards from Japan and India and England and Africa.

"Look at this one, will ya. You see that funny-looking building?"

"Sure."

"That damn thing is in Moscow, Russia."

"Wow!"

"God damn Russia."

All of the cards had the same tiny writing. None of them had stamps.

"Give her a call, will you Eddie," my father said. "I wouldn't mind finding out myself."

"Well, ain't that the shits."

Most Saturdays, just before the matinee, my father would drop me off in front of the Paramount, give me a dollar, and tell me he'd see me next week. After the movie, I'd walk back to the beauty shop and watch my mother sweep all the hair into neat, fuzzy piles.

"How's your father?"

"He's fine."

"He say anything?"

"Nope."

"Did he ask how we were doing?"

"Yeah."

"What did you say?"

"I said we were fine."

"What did he say?"

"Nothing much."

"What else did you do?"

"Got a haircut at Mr. Bertacci's. Went to the matinee."

"Poor Mr. Bertacci."

When I was twelve, the Main Street Theatre decided to do Lillian Hellman's *The Little Foxes*. My mother got a copy of the script, and, every night for two weeks, she practised the part of Alexandria until she knew most all the lines by heart.

"Who's Alexandria?"

"She's the ingenue lead."

"What's an ingenue?"

"A very pretty, young woman."

"That the part you want?"

Tryouts for the play were on a Thursday evening, and, even though it was a school night, I got to go and watch. My mother spent an hour combing out her hair. She tied it back with a yellow ribbon and put on her good white dress and heels.

There were about forty people in the auditorium, and one by one, they read lines from the play until Mr. Lipsitz nodded to them to stop. When it was my mother's turn, she strode to the front, dropped the script face down on a chair, and delivered Alexandria's lines until Mr. Lipsitz nodded and said thank you and called the next person.

"Did you hear what he said to me?"

"Who?"

"Mr. Lipsitz."

"You mean, 'thank you'?"

"No, he didn't say it that way at all."

"Does that mean you got the part?"

"Alexandria is supposed to be young and blonde and beautiful."

My mother wasn't blonde, and she didn't get the part. Betty Morehouse, who taught part-time at the high school, got to play Alexandria. I didn't even know my mother had gotten a part in the play until the day I came home from the Saturday matinee and found her in the back of the shop practising lines.

"You get a part?"

"Yes."

"I thought Miss Morehouse got the blonde part."

"She did."

"What part did you get?"

"Mr. Lipsitz asked me to play Regina."

"Is it a good part?"

"It's the female lead."

"So that's good."

"That's good."

When I saw my father that Friday, I told him about my mother getting the part in the play.

"She going to get to play a heroine?"

"What's that?"

"Heroines are women who believe all their dreams will come true."

"Are heroines like ingenues?"

"Ingenues? What the hell is an ingenue?"

"They're pretty women, blondes mostly."

"Your mother's no blonde, I can tell you that."

"Can we go see the play?"

"Where the hell did you get a word like *ingenue*?"

I offered to help my mother with her lines, but she said, no, she'd better do it herself. I asked her if I could come and watch the rehearsals, but she said that it would keep me up too late. She wouldn't even let me read the script.

"I thought you liked to see me read."

"I do, honey."

"Well, then, let me read the script."

"You wouldn't understand it."

"Has it got sort of naughty stuff in it?"

"Is that what your father told you?"

My grandmother lived just out of town. She had a small house, a chicken coop, and a large garden. Whenever we went to visit, she would take me out to the garden, and I would help her gather up potatoes and squash and corn and beans.

"You like squash yet?"

"Not much."

"You'll get used to it."

She kept the chickens in a small wire coop that stood off the ground on stilts. There were layers, she told me, and there were meat birds. These were meat birds.

"I don't like chicken all that much anymore, Granny."

"No profit in being a romantic."

"No, I mean, it sort of makes me gag."

"Light the candle and hand me that knife."

Afterwards, she would roll the carcasses over the flame until you could smell the burning feathers all the way in the house. Then she would scrub them down with soap and water, wrap them in brown butcher paper, and put them in the box with the vegetables.

"Granny, have you ever read *The Little Foxes*?"

"What is it?"

"A play."

"A play?"

"Mum's got a part in a play. It's the lead . . . Regina."

"Your father come around much anymore?"

"But Regina is not an ingenue."

"He still drink?"

The two of them had an argument. I got sent out to the garden, but I could hear my grandmother's voice, even over the crackle and snap of the cornstalks moving in the afternoon air. After we loaded the box into the trunk, my mother stood behind the car and looked at the house. She stood like that for a while, and, then, we got in the car and drove home.

Most Fridays my father would take me to Jerry's for dinner. I'd always order the cheeseburger and fries, and my father would order the clubhouse with a side of Thousand Islands dressing so he could dip his sandwich in it.

"You ever going to come home?"

"Ask your mother."

"She says you aren't."

"She should know."

I waited until he finished his sandwich and was stirring the sugar into his coffee.

"Mum said I could come to one of the rehearsals if you would take me."

"She said that?"

"Sort of."

"What did she say exactly?"

"I forget."

My father finished his coffee. He didn't say anything

else about the play, and I knew enough to keep my mouth shut. So I was surprised when we pulled up in front of the auditorium.

"Come on," he said. "Let's see what she's up to."

He told me to be quiet, that we were only going to stay for a little while. We stood at the back of the auditorium where it was dark and no one could see us. My mother and Miss Morehouse were on stage, and they were arguing. We watched the play for about fifteen minutes, and then my father nudged me. When we got out to the parking lot, he laughed suddenly and threw his head back.

"God, what a bitch!"

"Mum's pretty good, isn't she?"

"Just like real life."

"Can we go to see the play?"

"Wouldn't miss it for the world."

My father made me promise that I wouldn't tell my mother that we saw part of the rehearsal, and I didn't. But I did ask her if I could come to the play.

"You wouldn't enjoy it, honey."

"Sure I would."

"It's an adult play."

"If Dad takes me, can I come?"

"I'll talk to your father," she said. "Let me talk to your father."

My mother told my father that under no circumstances was he to bring me to the play. Those were her exact words, he said. We sat at the counter and ate our food in silence, and, when Jerry brought the coffee pot, my father asked me how old I was.

"Almost eleven."

"Well, hell," he said. "You're almost a man."

"Why doesn't Mum want me to see the play?"

"Because she's a bitch. In the play."

"It's just a play. It's not real life."

"Some people don't know the difference."

"I do."

"Good for you," and he slapped me on my shoulder. "Hey, Jerry," he shouted. "Bring my kid a cup of coffee, will ya. He's damn near a grown man."

"Does that mean we can go?"

I asked my mother once why they had split up and all she ever said was that marriage had been a surprise. I asked my father, too, but he said I should ask my mother. When I told him I had, he wanted to know what she had said. So I told him.

Friday was opening night. My father was waiting for me when I got to his apartment. He was dressed in a blue suit with a red tie. He looked real good.

"I got married in this suit."

"You look like a movie star."

"That's what your mother said."

We didn't go to Jerry's for dinner. We went to Antoine's instead, where you could sit at tables and have waitresses bring your food to you. My father spent the meal adjusting his napkin and looking at his watch.

"You think Mum could have been an actress?"

"All you need is a good imagination."

"Is that why you married her?"

"Is that what she said?"

We got to the auditorium late. I thought we would sit at the back where no one could see us, but my father marched down the centre aisle and found us seats in the second row.

If my mother saw us, she never let on. She was great. The character she played was an awful woman who was really nasty to Alexandria and who wouldn't give her husband his medicine when he was dying. By the end of the play, I was expecting that someone was going to shoot her. But no one did.

When the curtain came down, everyone in the auditorium stood and clapped, even my father. Then the players came out on the stage, and someone from behind the curtain brought out bouquets of flowers. Standing there in the lights, smiling at the applause, she really looked like an actress. She really did. My mother got two bouquets. Miss Morehouse only got one.

"So what did you think?" my father asked me as we walked to the car.

"She was good. Didn't you think she was good?"

"Made you want to strangle her, didn't it."

"She really wanted to play Alexandria."

"Alexandria? The blonde bimbo?"

* * *

My mother was waiting for me when I got home Saturday. She had put the bouquets of flowers in the green vase and set them in the shop window.

"Santucci throw those away?"

"No. I got them for being in the play."

"You must have been good."

"The big bunch is from your father."

We didn't talk about the play, and I was never sure if she knew I had been there. My father came by that Sunday still dressed in his suit, and the two of them went for a walk and talked, I guess. She came back alone.

My mother made lunch, and, while we were eating, she told me about how life was always full of surprises, that some of them were good and some of them were bad.

"Does that mean Dad is coming home?"

"What did I just say?"

Then she told me about Eddie Bertacci and the postcards. She was angry. I don't know why, but I figured it was because I had gone to the play. After lunch, she turned the hi-fi on and we listened to her records.

The flowers lost most of their petals in less than a week, but my mother trimmed and cut them back until there was nothing left but the stems.

The Garden Court Motor Motel

Sunday. And the train is late.

Sonny stands at the edge of the pool at the GARDEN COURT MOTOR MOTEL scooping bugs out of the water with the long-handled net and waits for the train to come chug-chug-chugging along. So he can hear Uncle HOLIE blow the train's horn. So he can wave to all the passengers on their way to the coast. Water in the pool is sure blue. Blue and cool. Maybe he'll take his shirt off. But he isn't going to get in. No, sir. No sky-blue water for him. Even if the clouds don't come and cool things off, he isn't fool enough for that.

He's the smart one.

There are three bugs on the net. Dead. All the bugs he pulls out of the pool are dead. When DAD was a boy, there were fish in the pool. That's what DAD says, and he knows everything.

Sonny knows everything too. He knows all about sky-blue pool water and dead bugs. You can't swim in the pool. You can't swim in the pool unless you rent a room.

Those are the rules, and ADAM and EVE and all their kids come by on vacation in a brand new Winnebago pull up to the office and say, pretty please, aren't going to get in the water until there's up-front money and the key deposit. That's the way things are.

Like it or hike it.

Sonny steps on a crack. Step on a crack, break your mother's back. Cracks in the concrete. Cracks in the white stucco. Cracks in the black asphalt. Cracks in the fifty-foot sign with the flashing neon-red ball that blinks "GARDEN COURT MOTOR MOTEL" and "Welcome."

And it's new.

Cracks in the windows. Cracks in the walls. Cracks hiding at the bottom of the pool where Sonny can't get at them.

Don't worry about the cracks, DAD tells Sonny. After a while, you don't even notice them.

The GARDEN COURT MOTOR MOTEL. Parking for long-haul truckers. Pool. Ice-making machine. Laundromat. Vibrating beds.

One day all this will be his. That's what DAD says.

The GARDEN COURT MOTOR MOTEL. Twenty-four rooms. Cable television. Telephone. Air conditioning. Video rentals. Breakfast coupons for the Heavenly Pie Pizza Palace.

Sonny swings the net deep and catches some cloud-shade on his shoulder. Here they come, he thinks to himself, and he forgets the bugs and looks up into the sky.

But it's not a cloud. There are no clouds. Not even on the edges of the world, which he can see clearly from poolside, is there even the mention of a cloud.

Now, what the DING-DONG is that, he says to the dead bugs in the net.

It's surely not a cloud. But now half of him is in the shade, and he's standing in shadows with his net and the dead bugs, watching the pool water turn black and deep.

Whatever it is, it's coming fast. And he starts thinking fast, too. A meteor would be okay. Or a flying saucer. Or a dark-green garbage bag.

One thing is for sure. It's not the train.

Okay. Okay. He looks up because he's run out of things, and he's sorry now he didn't finish high school.

"DING-DONG," he says, even though he knows DAD doesn't like that kind of language.

"DING-DONG," he says, because he's excited. Not in a naughty, excited way, but in that excited way he gets when he watches someone get whistled with a phaser on *Star Trek*.

"Clear the way!"

Doesn't sound like a meteor.

"Look out below!"

Doesn't sound like a green garbage bag.

"MOVE IT!"

And that's when Sonny thinks about running. Getting the DING-DONG out of there. And he knows now that this is the right answer, and that he would have thought of it all by himself if he had just had a little more time, but now it's too late, and he knows that whatever it is that is falling out of the sky and screaming at him is going to hit the motel or the parking lot or the pool or—DING-DONG, DING-DONG, DING-DONG—him.

Before he can finish netting all of the bugs.

The way DING-DONG hits the fan.

POOOWLAAASH!

The explosion whips the net out of Sonny's hands and knocks him off his feet, and, as he goes down in a wet, lumpy heap, he finally figures it out. The video camera was the right answer. He should have run and got the video camera.

DING-DONG!

Instead he didn't finish high school and that's sure as DING-DONG one of the reasons he's soaking wet, flat on his DING-DONG, watching the waves break over the side of the pool. His ears are ringing, but when he opens his eyes he discovers that he can see fine, and what he sees when he looks is something floating to the surface of the water.

It's too big to be a bug.

"Hello," says the woman. "Hello," she says again.

All Sonny can see is the woman's head, but what he sees is disturbing. RED SKIN and BLACK HAIR. Okay, okay, okay. Sonny has to think. BLACK PEOPLE have BLACK SKIN and BLACK HAIR. And ASIAN PEOPLE have YELLOW SKIN and BLACK HAIR.

This is hard.

And HISPANIC PEOPLE have BROWN SKIN and BLACK HAIR. So THE WOMAN WHO FELL FROM THE SKY must be . . . must be . . .

Sonny takes out his *Illustrated Field Guide for Exotic Cultures*, skips past Leviticus, and goes straight to the section with the pictures. Sonny thinks about asking the woman. Asking in a friendly manner. But he remembers that *asking is against the law*, and that if the WOMAN WHO FELL FROM THE SKY has the money or a valid credit card he is legally required to rent her a room. Unless the GARDEN COURT MOTOR MOTEL is all booked up, which it always is when people from exotic cultures arrive at the front desk.

But he can guess. Guessing isn't illegal. And after looking at all the pictures, some of which are pretty graphic and revealing, he guesses that the woman in the pool is an INDIAN.

"You have to be a guest to swim in the pool," says Sonny.

"What happened to all the water?" says the woman.

"That's the rule." And now Sonny's feeling better. Now he's feeling in charge, again.

"Last time I was here," says the WOMAN WHO FELL FROM THE SKY, "everything was water."

A meteor would have been simpler. Not the one that killed the dinosaurs. Something smaller. Dig it out, fill in the hole, patch the cracks, and get on with renting rooms to long-haul truckers bound for the coast. Too DING-DONG bad. Could have sold a meteor.

"What happened to the turtle?"

"We're all booked up," says Sonny.

"Why does the water smell funny?" The WOMAN WHO FELL FROM THE SKY gets out of the pool and

Sonny can see that his exotic culture tribulations are not over yet.

But Sonny has it figured out, now. The WOMAN WHO FELL FROM THE SKY fell out of a plane. You read about such things every day. She fell out of a plane. And the wind tore her clothes off.

That's why she's NAKED.

"DING-DONG," says Sonny, because he's excited and appalled at the same time.

"DING-DONG," he says again, because he didn't finish high school and can't think of anything else to say.

But most of all, Sonny says "DING-DONG" twice because the WOMAN WHO FELL FROM THE SKY has really big YOU-KNOW-WHATS and she's really hairy YOU-KNOW-WHERE.

And because she's PREGNANT.

Sonny looks up in the sky. But he doesn't see any sign of her INDIAN husband on the way down. Maybe he wasn't on the plane. Maybe he's driving out to meet her. Maybe he's on horseback. Maybe he's chasing buffalo. Maybe he's annoying a settler. Sonny knows what INDI-ANS do when no one is looking.

"You can't wait here," says Sonny. "You'll have to wait for him at the Heavenly Pie Pizza Palace."

"Who?"

"Your husband."

"What husband?"

DING-DONG, thinks Sonny. He was afraid of that. How many times has DAD warned him about something like this? As if there weren't enough women in the world already. As if we needed another one. And an INDIAN one at that. And PREGNANT at that. Well, she can't go to the Heavenly Pie Pizza Palace. Now that Sonny thinks about it, he remembers that people eat there. People bring their families there.

"We're all booked up."

"There's supposed to be a turtle," says the WOMAN WHO FELL FROM THE SKY, and she crosses her arms on top of her tummy and underneath her YOU-KNOW-WHATS, so the water drips off THOSE OTHER THINGS. "Where are all the water animals?"

Turtles? Water animals? Sonny doesn't like the sound of this.

"Who's going to dive into the water and bring up the dirt?"

All right! That does it. Sonny drops the pole by the side of the pool so it makes a CLANG-CLANG sound and gets the woman's attention.

"Dirt?" says Sonny. "Do you see any dirt at the bottom of my pool?"

The WOMAN WHO FELL FROM THE SKY walks to the edge of the pool and stares into the sky-blue water. And she looks at the GARDEN COURT MOTOR MOTEL. She doesn't look too happy now. She doesn't look too smug, either. Now she knows who's in charge.

"Not again," says the WOMAN WHO FELL FROM THE SKY.

"As for any animals," says Sonny, "there's a pet-damage deposit of twenty-five dollars, cash or credit card," though

Sonny doesn't know why he says this, since he can see that the WOMAN WHO FELL FROM THE SKY doesn't have any animals, nor does she have any pockets in which to keep a credit card or enough money for a pet deposit, let alone a room.

It's a good thing Sonny's already made the beds and vacuumed the office and checked the licences on the cars in the parking lot against the registration forms. It's a good thing he's collected the money from the vending machines and the washing machine and the dryer. It's a good thing he has nothing better to do than to stand by the pool and chat with an INDIAN who is NAKED and PREGNANT. It's a good thing DAD is having a nap. It's a good thing there's nothing on television.

"Why do you guys keep messing things up?" says the WOMAN WHO FELL FROM THE SKY. "Why can't you guys ever get things right?"

Sonny isn't sure the WOMAN WHO FELL FROM THE SKY knows the difference between right and not right. For instance, being NAKED is certainly not right. Being PREGNANT without a husband is definitely not right.

And being INDIAN . . . well, Sonny isn't positive that being an INDIAN is not right, but . . .

"Looks like we're going to have to fix it again," says the WOMAN WHO FELL FROM THE SKY.

We? What do you mean *we, Kemo-sabe?* DAD taught him that one. No way, Jose. Sonny knows them all. *Hasta la vista,* baby. Take a hike.

"Before it's too late."

Sonny knows better than to fall for that one. Only thing late around here is the train.

"Okay," says the WOMAN WHO FELL FROM THE SKY. "Pay attention. Here's how it's supposed to work. I fall out of the sky into the water and am rescued by a turtle. Four water animals dive to the bottom of the water and one of them brings up a bunch of dirt. I put the dirt on the back of the turtle and the dirt expands until it forms the Earth. Are you with me so far?"

DAD says that people who sound as if they know what they are talking about are generally trying to sell you something.

"Then I give birth to twins, a right-handed twin and a left-handed twin. They roam the world and give it its physical features. Between the two of them, they help to create a world that is balanced and in harmony."

Encyclopedias. Sonny is pretty sure that the WOMAN WHO FELL FROM THE SKY is selling encyclopedias.

"But if I can't find the turtle, I can't fix the world."

The train doesn't pull onto the siding next to the GARDEN COURT MOTOR MOTEL until evening.

"Three guys in a Chevrolet stalled on a level-crossing," Uncle HOLIE tells Sonny. "Drunk as skunks. Where's your DAD?"

"Sunday," says Sonny. "He's resting."

Uncle HOLIE and Sonny find the WOMAN WHO FELL FROM THE SKY a nice window seat.

"As soon as I find that turtle," says the WOMAN

WHO FELL FROM THE SKY, "I'll be back."

Uncle HOLIE and Sonny stand by the side of the train and watch the sun set. "Don't worry," Uncle HOLIE tells Sonny, as he signals the engineer and steps onto the caboose. "It's what DAD would do. And there hasn't been a turtle on the coast for years."

Sonny watches the train chug-chug-chug off into the night, the lights of the caboose swaying in the dusk. Then he walks back to the GARDEN COURT MOTOR MOTEL. With its twenty-four air-conditioned rooms. Cable television. Ice machine. Vibrating beds. Breakfast coupons for the Heavenly Pie Pizza Palace.

Sonny gets a soft drink from the vending machine and stretches out on one of the aqua-green plastic chaise longues by the pool and closes his eyes. Fix the world? Just as well the WOMAN WHO FELL FROM THE SKY couldn't find a turtle, he thinks to himself. Just as well she didn't have a credit card.

The white stucco of the motel plumps up pink and then blue as evening spreads out across the land, and the big neon ball that says "GARDEN COURT MOTOR MOTEL" and "Welcome" twinkles like a star in the western sky.

Not Counting the Indian, There Were Six

Auntie Beth was the scandal in our family. Before her death in a scuba-diving accident, she had had seven husbands. Not counting the Indian, there were six. Granny preferred not to count the Indian, because Beth and Juan "Kid Savage" McTavish were married in Mexico. It was an Indian ceremony; Beth sent back pictures but there was no doubt in Granny's mind about the legitimacy of a "pow-wow" as she called it.

"Can't call that a marriage," she said.

Then, too, Granny wasn't at all sure that Juan was really an Indian. She had lived a long time, she said, and she was sure we had killed off all the Indians.

"He's probably just a Mexican," Granny said.

According to the postcards Beth sent, Juan was a Kickapoo, part of a tribe that had fled the U.S. in the 1800s. Phoebe brought home a book from the library and, sure enough, the Kickapoos were in it. Granny just shook her head.

"I'm sure we killed them, too."

Juan was a professional boxer as well. "He fights for

Kickapoo culture," Beth wrote. All the money he made in the ring, she explained, went back to the tribe and that was why they were too poor to travel and why Beth loved him. It was the kind of nobility you found in new novels and old poems, and Granny snorted whenever Beth started about sacrifices and commitments. Beth wrote several times to say that she and Juan were coming to visit, but they never did.

One year later, Beth left noble causes and Juan and Mexico, and took up with a Chinese architect in Seattle. She married three more times before she died, floating up in the Gulf and leaving a string of stories, no children, and two and a half million dollars in her wake.

None of us knew about the money until after she died, and we were all summoned to court and given our share of her estate. After that, Auntie Beth was toasted as "eccentric" rather than "crazy" and "headstrong" rather than "self-indulgent." And all of the Auntie Beth stories were slowly resurrected from the family vault, polished and passed around at dinners as a memorial to the strength of the woman and a testimony to the power of cash. It was mostly the men in the family who drank to her health.

Granny endured the stories, but she endured them poorly, interrupting whenever Geraldine or Phoebe began romancing Beth and her penchant for "minor eccentricities."

"She wasn't eccentric, Phoebe," Granny would say. "She was a silly girl."

"Oh, no," Phoebe would whine. "Auntie Beth was just modern."

"Fiddle," said Granny.

On land, perched high in her floral wingback chair, Granny looked like a prehistoric bird, one of those dinosaur things, half reptile, with their long, jagged beaks and their ancient leather wings. Her hands were hooked claws which she clutched tightly in her lap, so you couldn't see the danger. But in the ocean of life, she was a leviathan sunk comfortably in the depths, looking up with black, bloodless eyes, watching the rest of us float around above her.

"Married six times," Granny would say, suddenly, and shake her head.

"Seven times, Granny," Geraldine or Phoebe would correct.

"Just looking for attention."

Granny had married once. There were eight children and a big house and Grandpa's whiskey. Geraldine said that Grandpa started drinking one night and raised his hand to hit Granny. "Uncle John said he didn't hit her, just raised his hand. When he realized what he had done, he was filled with remorse and began to cry." However, Aunt Ruth told us that Grandpa had hit Granny, knocked her down and that he only stopped because he was too drunk to continue. In Uncle John's version, Grandpa, blinded by tears, tried to sit down on a straight-backed kitchen chair, lost his balance, fell, and broke his arm. Aunt Ruth said that after Grandpa stopped hitting her, he collapsed in the easy chair and fell asleep and Granny went to the kitchen, took down a ten-inch cast-iron skillet, and broke his arm with it.

Whatever happened, Grandpa's arm was in a cast for two months and the next year, when Aunt Ruth graduated from high school, Grandpa moved out of the house (if you listened to Uncle John) or was thrown out (if you believed Aunt Ruth). He rented a small apartment above the firehouse and was found that winter, frozen in a hard lump behind the Chinese laundry, dead of a broken heart or dead drunk.

After that, Geraldine said, Uncle John said Auntie Beth started doing all sorts of crazy things. "It was because Auntie Beth loved Grandpa and she hated Granny for killing him." Aunt Ruth said Auntie Beth just liked being different. "Beth and Granny would always have these long talks about life," Ruth told us. "Those two were too much alike. You could see it." Uncle John said he could hear Beth and Granny arguing all the time, shouting. "Granny didn't like Beth doing the things she did, but Beth would tell her to go to hell and do them anyway."

There was occasional agreement in these stories. When Beth was eighteen, Granny put her out of the house. Homer Pyre saw Beth and Harold Loften holding hands in the theatre and called Granny. Harold was black and/or a criminal and Granny was a racist and/or concerned. Beth said she did it just to see what Granny would do and what Granny did was to pull all of Beth's clothes out of the drawers and wad them into three suitcases and place the cases on the front lawn. There was an envelope taped to the side of the large green one. Inside was a note, a bus ticket to Roseville, one hundred miles away, and a cheque for fifty dollars.

"Here are your clothes," the note said. "Please leave town."

So Auntie Beth left. Three years later, she came back with her first husband. He was a dentist in a three-piece blue suit with a blue shirt and a blue tie. He brought a bouquet of yellow flowers and a bright pink box of Granny's favourite candy, large, white-and-red-striped, hard-shelled peppermints. Phoebe and Geraldine took turns bringing in tea and listening at the door.

"He just sits there and goes on and on about teeth and what a nice house this is."

That evening, Beth and her dentist husband went back to San Francisco, and, when we got up in the morning, there were three suitcases on the front lawn. Phoebe and Geraldine opened the note that was taped to the side of the large green one. There was a cheque for fifty dollars and a note that said simply, "Having a wonderful time, wish you were here."

We brought the suitcases inside and Geraldine gave Granny the note.

"Wasn't that dentist fellow of Beth's nice?" Geraldine said.

Granny's eyes crackled, and the shawl covering her hands moved.

"He was so polite and well-dressed. That was a very modern tie."

Granny grunted and said something that sounded like "guppy."

And so the procession of "guppies" began. Every few years, Beth would bring another by, and Granny would sit in her chair, pass the candy dish, and watch them with the casual purpose of a hungry animal.

"Beth certainly lives an exciting life," said Phoebe over supper. "All those men and all that travelling."

"Those aren't men," said Granny. "Please pass the turkey." And Granny stabbed a big piece of white meat. "Was probably better off with the Mexican."

Between the marriages, Beth would come home alone. Sometimes she would just stay in her room. After her fourth marriage, when she was at the house, Geraldine and Phoebe and I sneaked down the stairs and listened at the door to the big room.

"You're looking well," said Granny. "Any children?"

"I'm not married right now."

"Oh," said Granny.

"I've met a very nice man, though. I think you'll like him."

"Of course. What happened to the Mexican?"

"You mean the Kickapoo."

"I mean the Mexican."

"Did you ever meet Bill?"

"Who's Bill?"

Sometimes when Auntie Beth came home, she would take my sisters and me to the park, and we'd play on the swings and talk.

"Have you been to Tahiti?" Beth would ask.

Of course, we hadn't, but Auntie Beth had, and she told us all about the sand piled up at steep angles on the beaches and the coral reefs alive with dark eels and bright fish and the sunsets all pink and glowing.

"Have you ever been skydiving?"

We said we didn't even know anyone who had done that.

"I've done that, too," said Beth. "You have to wear goggles because the wind blows so hard up there. And it's scary when you first step out of the plane and you begin to fall. Sometimes you wonder if your chute will open, but mostly you feel as though you could float forever like you were in an inner tube on the ocean. You just rock back and forth up there. My instructor says that some people enjoy the sensation so much that they just forget to open their chute."

Auntie Beth had done everything. She had gone canoeing down the Coppermine River in Canada and had surfed in Australia. She had been to Hawaii twice and climbed a volcano. She even had her own pilot's licence, and she could speak French and Spanish.

"Why'd you get married so many times?" Geraldine asked her once.

"Looking," said Beth.

"For what?"

"The right man, I guess."

"Why'd you marry all those wrong ones?"

"They didn't seem wrong at the time," Beth laughed.

"What was the Indian like?" said Phoebe.

"He was the best," said Beth.

"Granny doesn't have a man anymore, and she isn't looking," said Phoebe.

"Granny doesn't need a man," said Beth.

"Do you need a man?" said Geraldine.

Granny and Beth had a big fight after Beth brought home her sixth or seventh husband, depending on how you were counting. He was an artist with short spiky hair and red glasses. He smoked long, thin, black cigars, and, when Granny had Geraldine get him an ashtray and a plastic bag, he picked at the side of his nose, looked over his red glasses, and said, "What's the bag for, lady?"

"It's for your smelly butt," said Granny and she leaned out of her chair, ready to float over to the couch and chew on his head.

Later that night, Beth came back without her husband and she and Granny sat across from one another in the big room. For a long time, neither of them said a word.

Finally, Beth said "You'll be dead soon, why don't you try being nice?"

"I am nice," said Granny.

"Why do you hate me?"

"I don't hate you."

"You've never liked any of my husbands."

"I never met the Mexican."

"What about the others?"

"I'm very fond of you."

"You don't even let us stay in your house overnight."

"You can stay whenever you like," said Granny.

There was another silence. Beth sat on the couch. Granny sat in her chair.

"I don't think you love me at all."

"I love all my children."

"Robert says you're an old shark," said Beth.

"Who's Robert?" said Granny.

The next morning, Beth was gone. None of us ever saw her again. The postcards continued to come, but there weren't any more husbands. She sent us a postcard from Alaska and one from American Samoa. We looked up each place on the globe that Granny kept in the living room.

About two years later, we received a letter from the Galveston sheriff's office that said that Beth had died in a scuba-diving accident in the Gulf of Mexico. She had gone too deep, the letter said, and just ran out of air.

Phoebe was sure Beth had gone back to Mexico to be with Juan. "Isn't that romantic," said Phoebe. "She was looking for him when she died."

"What was she doing looking for him underwater?" snapped Granny.

But Phoebe was adamant, and maybe that's what Beth was looking for after all, for Juan. Looking down into the warm waters past the smaller fish, down to where the blue plunges into darkness and great shadows float slowly in the depths. And maybe it was Granny she saw just before her lungs burst.

Another Great Moment
in Canadian Indian History

Until Chief Justice Gordon Steels and the rest of the British Columbia Supreme Court decided that Owen Allands could not hunt on band land because Native rights in the province had been extinguished somewhere in the nineteenth century, the main topic of conversation in Fort Goodweatherday centred on why the town did not appear on any of the provincial road maps.

Amos Mischief insisted that it was because Fort Goodweatherday was an Indian community and wasn't worth the ink. Everett Joe said it was because the name was too long to squeeze in alongside the names of the larger towns along the coast.

There was an "FG" on the map, stuck out in the ocean, and this could have been Fort Goodweatherday, but as Fort Gregory and Fort Gustave and Fort Godspeed were in the same vicinity, it could just as well have been them, too.

"The 'FG'," Wilma Tom said each time the discussion about why Fort Goodweatherday wasn't on the map came up, "marks the spots where the fishing is good." It was an old joke. Wilma's grandfather had told it all his life and everyone knew it, but because really funny jokes were hard to come by, and because Wilma could tell a joke better than most people, nobody minded hearing it again.

Amos Mischief didn't have a great deal of time for jokes and whenever he got wound up about Fort Goodweatherday and discrimination and bigotry, Bella Tewksbury, who voted Reform in the last election and didn't mind telling you, would jump in and point out that Point Waboose, Grimsley, Lacoose, Russian Sound, and Pilgrim's Passage weren't on the map either. And all of them, with the exception of Lacoose, were larger than Fort Goodweatherday.

"Russian Sound even has a post office," said Bella. "What do you think about that?"

A year ago, Siv Darling, who was known up and down the coast for his bluntness, wrote a letter to the Minister of Tourism in Victoria and asked him why the town wasn't on the map. "Why isn't Fort Goodweatherday on the provincial road map?" the letter read. "Sincerely, Siv Darling."

Four months later, a package from the Minister of Tourism came back. Inside were a guide to the provincial parks, a guide on where to go in Victoria and Vancouver, and a glossy magazine that arranged, by months, all the exciting things to do in the province. There were a dozen pamphlets that offered two-for-one deals on meals and tours, discounts on hotel accommodations and car rentals, a colour postcard of a bunch of totem poles, a bumper sticker that said, "Visit Victoria," along with a really nice map of the province, which, sure enough, didn't have Fort Goodweatherday on it either. There was a letter stuck on top of everything that thanked Siv for his interest in visiting British Columbia and hoped his stay would be a pleasant one.

So Owen Allands was in no mood to hear Chief Justice Steels tell him and the world that all the treaties and agreements made between Native peoples and the province were null, and forthwith abrogated. Owen was found guilty of trespass on Crown lands and was sentenced to six months in jail, but after he took the time to explain just where Chief Justice Steels could put the court's decision, Owen's stay in jail was extended to nine months.

"Throwing Owen in jail like that was a bit much," said Everett Joe. "What the hell did the judge expect him to say?"

Bella brought a dictionary to the council meeting that was called to discuss the Steels decision, but she couldn't find the word "abrogated" anywhere, partly because she was spelling it wrong, and partly because, as she was searching through the pages, she hit upon the word "abort," which looked close enough. Rather than forget about it or leave well enough alone, Bella read the definition and was drawn into a heated discussion on abortion, and, by the time everyone had a turn at the microphone, a second council meeting had to be called for the next evening.

The second meeting started off with an impassioned

plea by Father Maris, who alternated months between Fort Goodweatherday and Lacoose, to stay calm and let the authorities do their jobs. It was the same speech he had made when the band closed the logging road that ran between Gull Point and Nadir to protest the clear-cutting of tribal land and very similar to the one he gave when Jimmy Turman's son, Dustin, was found hanged in a cell in Campbell River.

It was not a long speech, and, after he had finished, he thanked everyone for their patience, and went home.

As soon as Father Maris was gone, Bella Tewksbury pushed her sleeves up and knotted her arms across her chest. She leaned forward on the chair and said in a very loud voice, "So, what are we going to do about this?"

For the next four hours, everyone in the council meeting took turns at the microphone.

Crystal Kingcome brought a box of three-by-five cards on which Crystal and her three girls—Sheri, Terri, and Mari—had written the eight hundred number of the Minister of Justice. Crystal urged everyone to call the number as often as they felt like it, and, if enough people called, it might do some good. Best of all, Crystal pointed out, the phone calls were free.

Everett Joe thought a trip to the United Nations in New York would do more good, and, because he had lived in Toronto during the war, Everett volunteered to head the delegation.

Siv Darling wanted to close the Gull Point road again.

At around one o'clock in the morning, Florence Skloot, who had been sleeping in the second row next to the radiator ever since Father Maris got up to speak, woke up, hoisted herself on her walker, and shuffled to the front of the room.

Florence was between eight-six and ninety-seven, depending on whom you talked to, and, even as a young woman, she had a reputation for speaking deliberately. But as she got older, everything had really slowed down until the distance between each word and gesture allowed that you could get up and go to the bathroom as Florence was sneaking up on the noun, and get back before she had found the verb.

There were several glasses and a pitcher of water on the front table and Florence took the largest glass, filled it and drank it, and filled it again. Then she began.

"I'm ashamed," she said, and she paused to catch her breath and take another drink. "All we ever do is complain."

This was as fast as anyone could ever remember Florence moving, and Johnny Whitehorse, who had been thinking about stepping outside and having a smoke, decided to put it off until later.

"Complain, complain, complain," Florence continued. "No wonder the white peoples don't like us anymore."

Florence leaned over her walker. "Those white peoples are like little kids, you know," she said. "They don't know any better. That's why they do these things."

Florence stopped there, and, frankly, no one knew what to say. And no one left. Everyone just sat and waited. Finally, Florence cleared her throat and shifted her weight.

"What we need to do," she said in a clear, strong voice, "is to give them a hand with their problems instead of always complaining about ours."

Florence pulled a handkerchief from the sleeve of her sweater and wiped her face and cleaned the sides of her mouth. "We got to show them how to be friendly and generous," she said. "We got to be the adults."

Florence drank another glass of water. "So, I am going to that town and give those white peoples some help," she said. And she sat herself back on the walker and shuffled to her seat.

As soon as Florence was settled, Bella Tewksbury stood up and looked around as if she was trying to locate a forest fire. "Damn it!" she said in a booming voice. "Florence is right. And I'm going to drive her to Victoria."

Bella balanced her hands on her hips and squeezed her lips together. "So," she said, "who else is coming?"

This led to about twenty minutes of grumbling and mumbling and arguing, but Bella stood there like a lighthouse in a storm and waited. Finally Lillian Armstrong got up and then Betty Tom and Phyllis Aubutt joined her. Before long, everyone was up and standing with Florence and Bella.

The next morning Amos and Wilma and Siv got on the phone and began calling around to relatives and friends to see if anyone else wanted to come along. Bella and her sisters and nieces made sandwiches and packed cans of pop and bottles of water into cardboard boxes.

Amos Mischief's daughter Laura lived in Victoria and Amos figured that she wouldn't mind putting up a few people at her place, but Bella said no, that they should treat the trip like a vacation and stay in a nice hotel. Whereupon Everett Joe began telling Bella about his two years in Toronto and the kinds of prices that he had had to pay for hotels.

"Some of the fancier ones like the Royal York and the King Eddie were fifteen to twenty-five dollars," Everett cautioned. "For one night."

"That was years ago," said Bella. "It's going to cost us a little more than that, even in Victoria."

"We should stop off and see Owen," said Wilma.

"He's in jail," said Amos.

"If I was in jail," said Wilma, "I'd sure want friends to stop by and say hello."

There was a festive atmosphere to the caravan of cars and vans and trucks that headed out of Fort Good-weatherday. Florence rode in the front seat of Bella's station wagon and as soon as they turned left at the Petrocan station and headed inland, Florence rolled up against the door and went to sleep.

Larry Pugent was on duty at the reception desk of the Empress Hotel and thought that the fifty or sixty Indians walking through the lobby in his direction were part of a tour from Nagoya, Japan, that was almost a day late. He quickly called Laura Okazaki to come to the front desk and give him a hand.

"*Ko-nee-chi-wa,*" said Larry, and he bounced his head a little the way he had seen Laura do it.

Bella looked at Larry and then she turned to Amos and Wilma and Florence and the rest of the people. "Jesus," she said, "any of you guys speak French?"

"*Oui, je parle français,*" said Larry, delighted that he wouldn't have to depend on Laura after all.

Bella leaned on the counter and smiled at Larry. "How about English? Anybody here speak English?"

"Yes," said Laura Okazaki, who had just finished talking long distance with the tour operator in Nagoya, "I speak very good English."

"Good," said Bella. "How much for a room?"

"Unfortunately," said Larry, "we're all booked."

"That was Nagoya on the phone," said Laura. "They've had to cancel the tour."

"So," said Larry, hardly missing a beat, "how many are in your party?"

"The whole lot," said Bella.

Larry smiled at Laura, opened a book, counted heads, and ran his finger down several columns of small print. Then he went to a calculator, added up a line of figures, and wrote a number down on a piece of paper that said "Empress Hotel, Victoria, British Columbia," at the top in gold lettering.

Bella looked at the figure. "That much?" she said.

"It's a world-class hotel," said Larry.

"For two weeks?"

"No," said Larry, "for each day."

*   *   *

Amos called his daughter who called her boyfriend Brian who called his cousin Gerald who, as it happened, was related to Bella by marriage. Gerald called Reuben Lefthand who ran a Native arts and crafts store on Fort Street.

Reuben's uncle, Gus, ran a trailer park about twenty minutes out of town on the way to Sooke and would have been happy to put everybody up except it was tourist season and the entire park was full.

"But I got some tents you can borrow," Gus told everybody.

"And I know just the place you can camp," said Reuben.

Reuben and Amos and George packed the tents in George's van and everyone drove back into town with Reuben in the lead.

"You think he knows what he's doing?" Crystal asked Bella.

"Hard to say," said Bella. "He's not from around here."

Which was partly true. Reuben's mother was Salish, but his father was Crow out of Montana.

"But I suppose," said Bella, "a person shouldn't hold that against him."

Reuben worked his way through town, down to the waterfront, and around to the far side of the quay. When he was in front of the provincial parliament buildings, he parked the car and got out.

"Here we are," he said. And he grabbed one of the tents and carried it up on the lawn.

"You sure we can all camp here?" said Bella.

"Sure," said Reuben. "All the protest groups do it."

"We're not a protest group," said Wilma.

"Some of them even build little houses out of wood and cardboard," said Reuben.

"What are we going to do for bathrooms?"

"See that over there," said Reuben, gesturing to a large greystone building at the head of the quay. "You can use the bathrooms in there."

"Is that a government building, too?" asked Amos, who was thinking he had seen that building somewhere before.

"No," said Reuben, "it's the Empress Hotel."

Later that evening, after Reuben and the men had set up the tents, two RCMP officers stopped in.

"You can't camp here," said the second RCMP officer.

"We're not camping," said Bella. "We're protesting."

"Protesting what?" said the first RCMP officer.

"The Steels' decision," said Amos.

"And Owen Allands being stuck in jail," said Everett.

The officers walked back to their car and talked for a while, and then two more cars came along. Before long there were eight police cars parked in front of the provincial buildings and close to sixteen provincial and RCMP officers talking on their radios and to each other and to tourists who had stopped to see what was happening.

Finally an RCMP officer walked over to where Bella and Florence and Amos and Everett and Wilma and the rest of the people from Fort Goodweatherday were waiting.

"Okay," said the RCMP officer, "do you have any drums?"

"Why?" said Everett, who still wanted to go to New York and was not completely happy about camping out.

"The last Native protest group had drums," said the officer. "They made a lot of noise and disturbed the tourists."

"We're here to help you people," said Florence.

"Appreciate it," said the officer, and she tipped her cap to Florence. "We can use all the help we can get."

Early the next morning, Reuben Lefthand showed up with a large thermos of hot coffee and a box of day-old doughnuts. Even Bella was impressed.

"I guess those people out in Montana know how to do things right, after all," she told Wilma.

"It's going to be a beautiful day," said Reuben. "Have you figured out how you're going to help?"

Everett waved a doughnut at the provincial building. "Since we're already here, why don't we take over a building or something and demand that they release Owen?"

"I say we close a road," said Siv.

"What did that judge say about Natives?" said Wilma.

"He said we lived short and brutish lives," said Reuben. "We've had about four or five protests about that already."

"There we go complaining again," said Florence.

"If we're going to demand anything," said Amos, "we should demand that they put Fort Goodweatherday on the map."

For the next hour, everyone sat around and drank coffee and ate doughnuts and discussed everything from the Supreme Court decision to what Wilma's daughter Thelma should name her newborn son. Everyone, that is, except Bella and Florence.

Bella and Florence were busy looking through the newspaper that Reuben had brought along with the doughnuts and the coffee, and you could tell by the way Bella rattled the pages as she snapped them open and shut that she was serious.

"So," said Reuben, "any plans?"

Florence folded up her part of the newspaper, leaned back in the folding chair, and helped herself to a doughnut. "It says here," she began, "that the city is having trouble with tourists."

"That's right," said Reuben.

"We have the same problem up north," said Florence.

Florence took a bite of the doughnut and then she took another bite. Bella handed her a cup of coffee, and Florence sipped at that for a few minutes. Nobody moved, and nobody said anything. Somewhere in the distance, you could hear a coordinating conjunction moving in Florence's direction.

"And," continued Florence, after she had finished the doughnut, "they can be real pushy and nosy."

Reuben waited for a while and then leaned forward. "The problem is the city has too many tourists," he said. "All the hotels are booked and you can hardly get a reservation at a restaurant."

"We had a reservation," said Amos, adapting one of his two favourite jokes to the occasion, "until that idiot judge opened his mouth."

"Okay," said Florence, and she hoisted herself onto her walker and began working her way down the grassy slope to the sidewalk.

Bella watched Florence for a moment. "Well," she said to the rest of the people from Fort Goodweatherday, "any questions?"

All things considered, it was amazing how fast Florence could move on her walker. Around the quay they went and past the Empress Hotel, which you couldn't see too well now because of the tour buses and the horse-drawn carriages that were parked in front.

"Where are we going?" said Everett, who was having a little trouble keeping up.

"Hey, look," said Amos, "are they taking pictures of us?"

Sure enough, as the procession headed into town, several tourists stopped and pulled out their cameras and their video recorders and began filming Florence and Bella and the rest of the people from Goodweatherday.

Florence ignored the cameras. She clumped along

past the boats in the harbour, up a short incline, past the Tourist Information booth, and straight on along Government Street until she got to a nice-looking bookstore with a stone stoop.

"All right," said Florence as she settled in against the stoop, "now we're going to show the white peoples just how friendly and helpful we can be."

Everyone stood around the bookstore and waited to see what Florence had in mind. And they didn't have to wait long.

Coming down the street, a man and a woman were walking along looking at an open map. As Florence and the rest of the Indians watched, the couple stopped and looked down a street, walked a little further, looked back the way they had just come, and then walked ahead some more. When they arrived at the bookstore, Florence eased herself off the stoop and cut them off with her walker.

"Pardon me," said Florence. "You peoples look lost. Maybe we can help."

The man smiled at Florence and the woman looked around nervously, as Siv and Amos and Everett and Reuben and Crystal and her three girls and the rest of the people from Fort Goodweatherday crowded in to watch Florence.

"No," said the man, "we're not lost. We're just looking . . . for something."

"So, what are you looking around for?" said Florence.

"Tell them, Jerry," whispered the woman, "don't be a hero."

"It's okay, Linda," said Jerry. "I've got this under control."

"Just tell them what they want to know."

"Tell us," said Bella, who was now standing shoulder to shoulder with Jerry. "Florence wants to help you."

"It's really nothing," said Jerry. "We were just looking for the Empress Hotel."

"That one is easy," said Florence.

"I have a map," said Jerry.

"Let me see that," said Amos, and he snatched the map from Jerry and turned it around, but it didn't have Fort Goodweatherday on it, either.

"Okay," Florence said to Jerry and Linda, "follow me." And she set out down Government Street at a healthy clip. Everyone from Fort Goodweatherday moved with her, and Jerry and Linda were caught up in the surge and carried along like logs in a flood.

"Now that's the way it's done," said Bella, after they had dropped Jerry and Linda off in front of the hotel and watched them scamper in.

Even Siv Darling agreed that it had been a nice thing to do.

"Come on," said Florence, and she started back into town. "Let's find another tourist to help."

The next morning, Reuben arrived with doughnuts and coffee just as the police were getting out of their cars. Florence and Bella were already up and sitting in lawn chairs in front of the tents, watching the boats in the harbour.

"You guys made the papers," said Reuben. And he dropped a copy of the newspaper in Bella's lap.

"Morning," said the policeman who was right behind Reuben. "Who's in charge of this protest?"

There was a picture of Florence and Bella and the rest of the people from Fort Goodweatherday on the front page of the newspaper with a headline that read, "Indians Harass Tourists as Part of Protest."

"We'd like to talk to your chief," said the second policeman.

Bella tried to read the article and look at the policeman at the same time. "Our what?"

"The man in charge of this protest," said the first policeman.

Bella snorted and said something to Florence in Salish that made Florence smile.

"I'm sorry," said the second policeman. "I don't speak French."

"There have been complaints," said the first policeman.

"That's all changed," said Florence. "We're not going to complain anymore."

"That's good to hear," said the second policeman, "and mind the flowers."

"The problem," said Bella, folding the newspaper and putting it on the grass, "is that they haven't seen friendly Indians in so long, they thought we were trying to create a disturbance."

"So what do we do?" said Amos.

"Smile," said Florence. "We got to smile more."

Wilma made up a list of ways you could be helpful, and, for the rest of the day, everybody from Fort Good-weatherday smiled as hard as they could as they helped the tourists in Victoria with their bags or took their pictures or offered directions or suggested restaurants or just took the time to ask whether or not they had heard about the decision that the Chief Justice of the British Columbia Supreme Court had made concerning Native land and Native rights.

Even Siv Darling smiled, which was a big concession for Siv since he seldom found anything to smile about.

Everyone was tired by the end of the day. "Helping is a lot harder than complaining," Amos told Crystal and her three daughters. "I hope Florence knows what she's doing."

The next morning, Reuben arrived just behind the television trucks and a dark sedan. The three men who got out of the sedan were dressed in casual slacks and pullover shirts with little animals stitched into the material just below the collar. Two of the men had knapsacks slung over their shoulders. The third man was tall and slim, and from the moment he stepped out of the car until he got where the people from Fort Goodweather-day were waiting for him, he was smiling.

"Oh, God!" said Bella. "University."

"Don't know," said Florence, selecting a doughnut from the box Reuben was passing around. "Could be government."

"Good morning," said the tall, slim man. "Welcome to Victoria."

The television crews pushed in, measuring the angles. They dragged their cameras and cables through the flower beds and up the rise, swirling around the men from the government like currents in a river.

"We understand what you're trying to do," said the tall, slim man, looking around the camp and nodding his head, "and we wanted to tell you that we're sympathetic."

Bella looked at Amos, and Amos looked at Wilma, and Wilma looked at Florence. The television lights were hot and bright, and Florence had to shield her eyes.

"But this isn't the way to do it," said the second man.

"No," said the third man. "In the end, people who are sympathetic with your cause right now will turn against you."

"We may lose a tourist or two," said the tall, slim man, "but in the end, the only people you'll hurt will be yourselves."

And the three men went around the camp and shook hands and asked everyone from Fort Goodweatherday questions such as where they were from and how they liked Victoria so far and whom they were pulling for in the playoffs.

After the men got back into their sedan and drove off,

and the television people packed up their cameras and cables, Bella leaned over to Florence.

"You were right," she said in a low voice. "Government. For sure."

The people from Fort Goodweatherday stayed on in Victoria and helped out as best they could, and, by the end of the week, the number of tourists in the city had dropped by forty-seven percent.

"It says here," said Bella, as she sat on the lawn of the provincial building and read an article in the newspaper over coffee and doughnuts, "that the British Columbia Supreme Court is going to reconsider Steels' decision."

"They going to let Owen go?

"You guys are something else," Reuben told Bella. "I've never seen the place so dead."

"Smiling and being helpful," said Florence, "is always better than complaining."

"It didn't put us on the map," said Amos.

"When are we going home?" said Wilma. "I've got a grandson needs naming."

Florence pulled herself onto her walker. The late morning sun filled the harbour and set the boats ablaze, and, from where she stood, Florence could see the Empress Hotel lying in the shade like a sleeping dog and the quiet streets that ran from town to the water and the information booth at the far side of the quay that hadn't been open for the past two days.

"Well," she said, "looks like we've done as much as we can."

The drive back to Fort Goodweatherday was uneventful unless you count the two flat tires Amos discovered when he came out of the restaurant in Campbell River or the shouting match Bella got into at a gas station with a woman who had recognized the people from Fort Goodweatherday from a picture in the paper.

"Some people are so proud," Bella told Wilma, "having to admit they need help makes them cranky."

The weather along the coast was unseasonably sunny, and when everyone arrived home, most of the news, with the exception of the salmon fishing season having been reduced by three weeks, was good. Thelma hadn't named her son yet, which made Wilma happy because Wilma wasn't sure Thelma was old enough to come up with a good name on her own.

"She was thinking of calling him Clarence," Wilma told Bella. "Good thing I got back in time."

The following week, Owen Allands was released from jail.

Amos remained unhappy about Fort Goodweatherday not being on the map, but as Bella was quick to point out, Victoria *was* on the map and look at the mess it was in.

"There were people everywhere," said Wilma. "That tourist thing is a little scary. Not sure I want everybody in the world knowing where I live."

At the next council meeting, Florence gave a report on the trip to Victoria and how helping other people with their problems had been the right thing to do.

"Should have seen the looks on their faces," Florence told everyone. "It's not something they'll soon forget."

"Course we can't be doing this all the time," Bella cautioned. "Being helpful is all well and good, but it's a long drive, and it we're not careful, we could create one of those cycles of dependency."

"Don't forget the provincial road map problem," said Amos Mischief.

Everyone at the meeting agreed with Bella and Amos.

"Helping was fun," said Wilma, who had decided that Barnes was a better name for her grandson than Clarence, "but eventually, those people are just going to have to learn to work things out for themselves."

Acknowledgments

These stories, with occasional variations, have been published and/or broadcast, as follows:

"A Short History of Indians in Canada" in *Toronto Life* and *Canadian Literature*; reprinted as "A Short History of Indians in America" in *Story* and broadcast on CBC's *Gzowski in Conversation* and Alaska Radio's *Air Traffic*; "Tidings of Comfort and Joy" in the *National Post* and broadcast on CBC's *Between the Covers*; "The Dog I Wish I Had, I Would Call It Helen" in *The Malahat Review* and *Journey Prize Anthology*; "Coyote and the Enemy Aliens" in *Our Story: Aboriginal Voices on Canada's Past*; "Little Bombs" in *West Magazine*; "Bad Men Who Love Jesus" in *New Quarterly*. "The Closer You Get to Canada, the More Things Will Eat Your Horses" in *Whetstone*; "Not Enough Horses" in *The Walrus*; "Noah's Ark" in *Descant*; reprinted as "Nuh'un Gemisi" in *Paralelin Ötesinde: Kanadali Yazarlardan Öyküler*; "Where the Borg Are" in *Story of a Nation: Defining Moments in Our History*; "States to Avoid" in

Parallel Voices; "Fire and Rain" in *Border Crossings*; "Domestic Furies" in *The Malahat Review*; "The Garden Court Motor Motel" in *Prairie Fire* and *The Nelson Introduction to Literature*; "Not Counting the Indian, There Were Six" in *The Malahat Review*; "Another Great Moment in Canadian Indian History" broadcast on CBC's *Between the Covers*; reprinted as "Another Great Moment in North American Indian History" in *Story*.

Thomas King is an award-winning novelist, short story writer, scriptwriter, and photographer. His many books include *Medicine River, Truth and Bright Water, The Truth About Stories* (Minnesota, 2005), *One Good Story, That One* (Minnesota, 2013), and *The Inconvenient Indian: A Curious Account of Native People in North America* (Minnesota, 2013). He is the author of several picture books for children, the editor of *All My Relations: An Anthology of Contemporary Canadian Native Fiction,* and coeditor of *The Native in Literature: Canadian and Comparative Perspectives.* He has a popular CBC Radio series, *The Dead Dog Café Hour.* He is professor of English at the University of Guelph, where he teaches Native literature and creative writing.